Praise for *Saltwater Cowboys*

". . . a hilarious and heart-rending tale that you'll read
and re-read. With pleasure."
—Loyd Little, author of *Parthian Shot*, winner of
the PEN Hemingway Award.

"The best fictional take on what's really happening on
Carolina's central coast since Margaret Maron's *Shooting
at Loons*. Catch this rowdy ride!"
—Bland Simpson, author of *Ghost Ship of
Diamond Shoals* and *Into the Sound Country.*

Bill Morris

Coastal Carolina Press
Wilmington, N.C.

 Coastal Carolina Press, Wilmington, NC 28403
www.coastalcarolinapress.org

© 2004 by Bill Morris.

First edition 2004.

ISBN: 1-928556-45-0.

08 07 06 05 04   5 4 3 2 1

Grateful acknowledgment is made to Reverend Rusty Willis for permission to excerpt a portion of his sermon, "The Pilot of Old" in Chapter 16.

Printed in the United States.

Applied for Library of Congress Cataloging-in-Publication Data.

Cover Design: Paula Knorr, Maximum Design + Advertising, Inc.
Book Design: Dorothy A. Gallagher.

For Debbie and Grace

In Greek mythology, the sea turtle represented the feminine power of water and was the emblem of the goddess of love, Aphrodite. It is Aphrodite who makes men babble and grow weak and lose their senses.

acknowledgements

The author wishes to thank the people of Down East Carteret County, whose rich history has been borrowed as the story behind this story. Although a few of the places in this book are real, none of the people or events are.

Research for this book included works by the two leading authorities on coastal North Carolina, David Stick and Dr. Orrin Pilkey, along with Charles H. Whedbee's *The Flaming Ship of Ocracoke and Other Tales of the Outer Banks* and Homer Hickam's *Torpedo Junction*. Less well known is Carteret County's own Melvin Robinson, whose alternative history, *Riddle of the Lost Colony*, is unfortunately long out of print. Special thanks to Reverend Rusty Willis of the Ann Street Methodist Church in Beaufort for permission to use an excerpt from his sermon, "The Pilot of Old." This list would be incomplete without acknowledging Nikki Smith, who as editor provided an enormous amount of help in a very short period of time.

saltwater cowboys

squall lines
a prologue

"A barrier island's no barrier a'tall. They couldn't keep out the English or the Spanish before them or the Yankees after them. They don't keep out hurricanes either, as anybody who was around for Hazel can tell you."

That's what my grandfather did tell me when I was only a boy, twenty years after Hurricane Hazel. In his eyes barrier islands—what we call "the Banks"—were nothing but a shifting string of sand castles that split the ocean and the sound into separate bodies bleeding into one another at inlets. They change shape, a grain at a time, according to the wind, waves, tides, and currents. Granddad knew what he was talking about; Professor Wayne Taylor Dodge studied the Banks for half his long life.

In the quarter century since Granddad pronounced them "no barrier a'tall," others have proven that those same sand islands are indeed no barriers when it comes to building condos, shopping centers, and motels. But for most of human history the Banks of North Carolina have harbored only impermanent settlements. The Native Americans went there for fishing but they sensibly built their villages on the mainland. The Europeans generally followed suit.

This story is about one of those soundside villages called Croaker Neck. The name is taken from a common type of fish with the uncommon ability to speak. Or at least croak. The croaker's name comes from the noise he makes, a guttural grunt much lower than a frog's. Caught on your hook or in your net, he makes that grunting sound as if you might think twice about throwing him in the ice chest. I read a book once about a talking flounder, but that was a novel and completely made up. This is real. Croakers do croak.

Our neck of land lies between No Name Bay and Ballast Creek, where the first permanent settlers found piles of ballast rock that had been left behind by the English sailors who'd been here long before. Today folks use the rocks to decorate around their hydrangea bushes or to prop open a shed door.

Most of the families in town are part of the Diamond City *diaspora*. Whales were the first creatures in these waters to be harvested for money, and a thriving village of whalers grew up at Cape Lookout, with livestock and barns, stores and a school. When the brick lighthouse went up in 1859 it was painted in black-and-white diamonds; the whaling village, already more than a century old, became known as Diamond City. Then came a succession of hurricanes and finally even the die-hards abandoned their village on the Banks. Many of them went to Harkers Island. Some went to a spot on the mainland that is to this day called The Promised Land. Other families migrated across to Gloucester or Marshallberg.

Croaker Neck, the legend goes, was settled by the last Bankers to leave. They were the most daring of the small-boat whalers, the offspring of blockade runners and privateers. "Hard crabs," the others called them. The whalers became fishermen, shrimpers, and gatherers of oysters and crabs. The ship's carpenters who built their boats built fine white houses, too, with porches shaded by native live oaks and other trees that bore figs and persimmons. The houses, mainly yellow pine, were built to last. Eventually they outlasted the hard crabs themselves.

I first came to Croaker Neck as a curious boy who couldn't hear enough of my grandfather's stories about hurricanes, shipwrecks and haunted islands in the sound. From my childhood until just recently those were still the tales most often told here. But then a new set of stories started to take shape, much as a squall line forms on the horizon. Surveyors were carving up the last of the big marsh islands. A New York movie director moved his studio into an abandoned crab house. Sea turtles began to show up in the strangest places . . . .

chapter one

Even in the dark the voyage from Croaker Neck harbor to the back side of Atlantic Beach can be made in less than an hour. But it was well past midnight when I tied the *R/V Gannet* up at the dock of the Binnacle Inn and JungleGolf and walked into the haze of yellow bug-bulb light. A squad of creosoted posts holds the motel box a story above ground level, and their criss-crossed shadows lay at odd angles on the sand-dusted concrete pad. In the center, a wispy cloud of steam rose from the surface of a sunken Jacuzzi.

Surrounding the tub, yellow crime-scene tape was threaded through several lawn chairs and tied off to the stainless steel handrails that humped above grade on one side of the human crockpot. In one of the chairs, a thin young woman sat red-eyed and shivering under a layer of flimsy motel towels. It was late May, and the night air still had enough chill to raise steam off a Jacuzzi or goose bumps off a white girl's skin. Three Atlantic Beach cops were hovering over her, one asking questions while the others tried not to stare too obviously at the margins of the towels. A fourth cop, a tall, thin Black guy wearing a baseball cap and a dark windbreaker with NOAA ENFORCEMENT stenciled on the back, was busy talking on his cell phone. At the front of the motel, the side opposite Bogue Sound, two EMT's were loading an occupied gurney into an Atlantic Beach Fire Department ambulance. The slamming doors caused the shivering woman to suddenly shudder. With siren blaring the ambulance headed off for the hospital in Morehead City.

After the siren faded I could hear the gentle noise of breaking surf. The Atlantic Ocean lay just across the street, hidden by the hedges in front of another motel. In the hole between two breakers, a familiar voice called my name.

"Dodge Lawson! What took you so long?"

I recognized Ilse Brunner by the fringe of red hair sticking out from under a baseball cap. Dressed in a stylishly slick nylon sweat suit, she was on one knee at the edge of the Jacuzzi, pouring ice from a bucket into the steaming water. Even in the yellow bug lights she looked good, the lines on her face inscribing a gently worn beauty that made women half her age seem like first drafts.

"Where have you been?" she demanded.

"Low tide. We have them twice a day, if you haven't noticed."

Ilse had phoned me shortly after ten, and I'd immediately set off in my boat, the *R/V Gannet*. The trip from my dock in Croaker Neck had taken under an hour, but a sand bar at the entrance to the motel's neglected boat basin forced me to wait for the incoming tide.

"You're paid to hurry," she said, still kneeling by the pool.

"Oh, absolutely." I crouched down beside her. "And I'm only in this for the money."

Ilse's dark eyes flashed. She started to say something, but

8

caught herself, knowing that it would be a waste of breath. With a shake of her head she went back to pouring ice, and making soothing noises toward the rising steam. When the cloud thinned near the surface I could make out a large, oblong shape afloat in the Jacuzzi.

"It will be all right for you soon," Ilse cooed. "My poor, poor *schatz.*" Her slightly accented voice flowed with the lilt of a children's book read aloud.

"What's with the ice?"

"To keep him from cooking, of course."

Through the steam I could see that the rounded shape in the pool was a quarter-ton of prehistoric reptile, a loggerhead turtle the *Gannet* and I would carry back to sea. His reddish-brown shell was about four feet long, and the rust-colored scales on top of his head were the size of slightly irregular playing cards. The prodigious embossing of barnacles on his shell gave the impression of an implacable strength, and I didn't think the animal was in any danger of cooking in a tub of lukewarm water.

But Ilse was cooing to him anyway, offering sympathy in two languages. As president of Tortugas Now! she is usually one of the first on the scene of any turtle stranding. The turtle hotline rings in her restored colonial house in the Beaufort historical district, three bridges and two centuries from the Binnacle Inn and the rest of the Atlantic Beach strip.

By virtue of having a boat with a crane—and knowing Ilse—I landed a contract with Tortugas Now! that pays me to pick up and move sick or stranded turtles. I've picked up most of my passengers in the sound, where boaters see them floating and call the hotline. I've also seen turtles stranded on the beach above the high tide line, where they can get stuck in a tire rut or a hole dug by some fun-loving tourist kids. In two years of carrying turtles on the *Gannet* I had seen them in some strange places—but I never thought I'd see a loggerhead in a Jacuzzi.

The cops finally took their eyes off the towel-clad young woman long enough to look over at me. Like Ilse, they didn't seem too happy with my tardiness. I asked her about the tall FBI-looking guy.

"He is a National Marine Fisheries policeman."

"Three dozen turtle rescues, I've never seen one of those before."

"Well, this stranding is sort of unusual, wouldn't you say?"

Just as I got up and started walking back to the dock the Fisheries enforcer snapped his cell phone shut and started staight over to me with a serious government-issue walk. His jet-black, made-for-walking brogans were shined to military standards. Trailing him was one of the regular beach officers, a guy I recognized from his off-duty job at the fuel dock on Radio Island. He moved with the bored shuffle of a beach-town patrolman all set to deal with a long summer of hassling loitering teenagers.

"This is Ron Gatlin," he said. The other guy picked it up from there, calling himself "the National Oceanic and Atmospheric Administration Fisheries Enforcement Special Agent in Charge." With the slightest of nods in my direction the Black guy pulled his jacket aside to show me a badge hung around his neck, also giving me a glimpse of the holstered automatic clipped onto his belt. He handed me a business card and as I was admiring the amount of type they had managed to squeeze onto it, just for his title, plus two office phone numbers and one for his cell, the Atlantic Beach officer—Snow, according to his nametag—

pointed a warning finger in my direction. A shred of what looked like coleslaw was stuck to the fingernail.

"Walk with me, Lawson," he growled, and we stepped away from the Jacuzzi. Gatlin looked like he was about to climb all over Snow for talking out of turn, but his cell phone started ringing and he turned around to answer it, rotating his body into that imaginary phone booth stance that habitual cell phone users deploy in a crowd.

"First of all," Snow said, with a nod in Ilse's direction, "save that low tide bullshit for the foreigners. And second—"

"Who's the G-man?" I interrupted.

"The federal pain in my worn-out ass. He's stationed in Carolina Beach, just happened to be up here inspecting shrimp trawlers. I guess he heard us calling this turtle deal into the Coast Guard on the radio."

"And the butt-naked suspect?"

"Suspect? Any suspect, it's the turtle. The girl's a teacher from Buncombe County. Down here with a busload of kids, learning about Blackbeard the Pirate."

"Arggghhhh, may-tee." It was a well-worn local joke, spoofing the Blackbeard trade, but his face unfroze into the faintest of cop grins, giving me the opening to ask, "So, who went off in the ambulance?"

"Her fellow field trip chaperone and skinny-dipper, a shop teacher named Earl. Earl has a bad case of bruised nuts."

"How'd that happen?"

"Turtle surprise," he said, pointing toward the Jacuzzi.

"Ouch. You saying the guy's nuts were hurt so bad you had to put him in an ambulance?"

"Asthma. Turtle goosed him and his asthma kicked in. When I got here he was turnin' blue."

Snow went on to tell me the whole story. According to the Buncombe teacher, after the kids were asleep the shop teacher Earl showed up at her motel room door carrying a six-pack of Tequiza. The two of them, young and at the beach, consumed four bottles of the tequila-flavored malt beverage, and soon she was giggling in the "courtyard" underneath the motel, watching as Earl stripped and began to lower himself into the bubbling whirlpool.

"Sounds like a love story to me."

"Naturally," Snow said, "good-ol' Earl went in backwards, so he wouldn't miss his date dropping her own drawers."

"Naturally," I agreed. In my mind was a picture of Earl, backing into the jet-powered water, savoring his malt liquor buzz as he watched his fellow chaperone unhook her bra and let it fall to the sandy concrete. The guy must have been very pleased with himself in those few exciting moments that ended when his ass first made contact with the probing overbite of the loggerhead's prehistoric snout. The poor sap had no idea who was lurking in the froth and steam, so maybe the first nudge only confused him. But there couldn't have been much room for doubt when the 500-pound turtle brought its bowling-ball head up sharply in the space between Earl's legs and gave him what nearly turned out to be the last goosing of his life.

"The shop teacher turned blue," Snow repeated, "and the woman started freaking out, running around naked yelling for somebody to call 9-1-1."

We both chuckled a little over that, but then Special Agent Gatlin walked up and Snow instantly quit clowning around. "Whoever it was put the turtle in the hot tub just missed a manslaughter charge by this much," he said, holding his thumb and forefinger up in front of my face.

"Not to mention a blatant violation of the Endangered Species Act," Gatlin chimed in.

"What makes you think somebody put the turtle there?" I wondered. "Couldn't it have just wandered in off the beach?"

"The turtle Nazi seems pretty sure about it." Snow used one of the local nicknames for Ilse Brunner. She had collected her share, and Turtle Nazi was far from the worst. I could see that the agent, a turtle professional himself, didn't care for the Nazi reference.

"The males don't beach themselves. They've got no eggs to lay, so they don't usually climb up on the beach."

"Well, y'all are the experts, and I'm just the hired hand."

"Look." Snow blew breath in my face that smelled like day-old chum. "I know you live in Croaker Neck, and the saltwater cowboys over there are ill with these turtle people. I figure that if somebody moved this turtle, you might have an idea who it was."

It was getting late and the bad cop-worse-cop routine was beginning to tire me out. "Are you going to have me keel-hauled?" I asked. "Or should I save the turtle?"

"Go ahead," Snow said, finally giving up the tough-guy act. "The damn thing probably just wandered in here anyway.

God damn these endangered species anyway!" he cursed, just as Ilse was walking up to us.

"Threatened," she corrected him in an even tone.

"What's that?"

"Loggerheads are a threatened species. The leatherbacks, Kemp's Ridley, the hawksbill, and green turtles are endangered."

"Well, God damn them all anyway!"

The color rose in Ilse's face, like she was about to pop a gasket. I'd seen that look many times before. There was no denying that high dudgeon looked good on her.

"Do you always swear at the victim of a crime?" Then she started tearing into poor Snow in a shrill voice just as familiar to me as the soothing tone she'd been using on the turtle. I turned from both of them and walked back to where I'd left the *R/V Gannet* tied up at the Binnacle Inn's poor excuse for a dock.

The *R/V* designation on my boat means that she is a research vessel, not a recreational vehicle. Years ago my grandfather took the name, *Gannet,* from the elegant black-and-white seabirds that nest in Iceland and winter here on the North Carolina Banks. My boat's color-scheme is essentially the same as the birds', even though the white may be more of a dull gray, and a greenish growth discolors the black bottom paint below the water line. She's a wooden boat built in the side yard by one of those home-grown geniuses on Harkers Island. In style she is "vernacular," designed by the shipwright's eye, wide in the beam, round at the stern, and made entirely of juniper and yellow pine. Just under thirty feet, with the distinctive Core Sounder's round stern and flared bow, she began life as a shrimp trawler, then at some point was converted over to sink netting. The original windlass remains, but my grandfather had her rigged with a davits, a sort of nautical crane to make a functional, if low-budget, research vessel. Granddad taught me how to pilot the *Gannet* when I had to stand on an overturned bucket to see past the top of the wheel.

On my watch, she's never been used for research. In addition to getting paid for rescuing turtles, the *Gannet* and I engage in blue-collar work like building docks, repairing docks, and retrieving mangled docks left in the wake of nor'easters and hurricanes. The turtle work pays best, though. There's never a lack of donations to Tortugas Now!

To get Ilse out of his face, Snow escorted the shaken teacher back to her motel room. When he returned it was time to move the loggerhead. That would require some wading, and soon the cops—but not the Special Agent—were stripping down to their skivvies and bitching a blue streak. The muttering suddenly stopped, though, when Ilse began to take off her clothes. She had a few years on the oldest of the lawmen, but they all went temporarily mute at the unveiling of the sleek turquoise one-piece bathing suit that had been hidden beneath her Nike nylon. With their undivided attention firmly in hand, she slipped into the lukewarm Jacuzzi and took charge.

Working together, the four of them slipped a ballistic-cloth sling under the docile turtle. I boomed the *Gannet's* crane as far as I could and then paid out enough cable to get a hook connected to the eye of the sling. With Ilse guiding, I worked the control levers to gently lift the turtle out of the hot tub and onto a wheeled cart. From there it was a simple matter to ease him over to the dock and down onto my deck.

Soaked to their waists, the deputies renewed their bitching and went off to wring out their boxers. Gatlin kept busy taking pictures with a small digital camera and making notes in a spiral-bound tablet. The super-efficient way he went about his business made me think he had to be new, doing his job with rookie enthusiasm. This mistake—a misunderestimation, as one of our recent Presidents might say—was one I'd soon come to regret.

With me and her precious turtle on board, Ilse untied my dock lines and tossed them on deck. "You be careful," she said, shoving me off. They could call her a foreigner if they wanted, and worse than that, but I knew few people who were better around boats than Ilse. Not too long ago, she would have been eager to follow the dock lines aboard and take the ride with me, out Beaufort Inlet and into the ocean, to the secret spot we'd picked to release the turtles. Now I'd have to make that trip alone, knowing that her words of care were meant more for the *Caretta caretta* on my deck than for me.

"Good night," I called, drifting away from the dock. But she was already beyond hailing distance, gathering up her clothes from the pool apron.

The *Gannet's* Detroit Diesel beat its clanking machine-gun rhythm as we motored up Bogue Sound and into the turning basin at Morehead City. A brightly lit and spotless Japanese freighter was tied up at the state port, taking on a load of wood chips, our state's decidedly low-tech but largest export. It's not the first time North Carolina's forests have been cut and shipped—British shipyards depended on our naval stores, but Yokohama is a lot farther away than Bristol.

Across the channel from the freighter a rusting Nassau-registered tanker pumped aviation fuel into the tank farm on Radio Island. The jet fuel would travel by truck or barge to the nearby Marine Corps Air Station at Cherry Point, where it would power Harrier jets and F-4s.

Leaving the port, I turned south into the shipping channel and Beaufort Inlet, generally considered the southern boundary of the Outer Banks. At the Fort Macon Coast Guard station my loggerhead buddy and I passed the daunting shape of a cutter preparing to go on patrol. To seaward were only the blinking red and green lights of the channel buoys against the endless black of the Atlantic Ocean at night.

Clear of the bars near the inlet, I turned between two red buoys and headed east-southeast, following a familiar course three miles off Shackleford Banks. The ocean was calm, or "*slick cam,*" as they say. The sturdy *Gannet* barely rolled as a gentle swell passed under her keel.

Other than a few fishermen's lanterns, the only light source I could see was the revolving beacon of the Cape Lookout light. The first rickety wood-and-brick version had been lit in 1812, but it was too short and its light too weak, and it was replaced in 1859 by the sturdy brick tower, 150 feet tall, that still shines its light as far as twenty-five miles out to sea. While any school child can name Cape Hatteras, and any movie buff knows Cape Fear, few who haven't been here are even aware of Cape Lookout's existence. The early Spanish charts called it Cape Trafalgar, after a point on the coast of Andalusia. When the Italian Giovanni Da Verrazzano got here, on the Feast of the Annunciation in 1524, he named it Cape Annunciata. Later it became *Promontorum Tremendum,* until more literal-minded English mapmakers substituted Cape Look Out.

Watching the lighthouse blink, I began to wonder who might have put a turtle in the motel Jacuzzi. Threatened or not, there seemed to be plenty of loggerheads in Core Sound and the nearby ocean, so catching one would not have been all that difficult. But keeping it alive, and sneaking it under the motel, would take some doing.

I knew that Ilse was right, there was no way the loggerhead had somehow wandered ashore on its own. And definitely not a male loggerhead, because that would go against Nature, and the sea turtle is one of Nature's favored creatures. They evolved in the Upper Triassic, before the dinosaurs, and they are still with us long after their oversized reptilian cousins departed the scene. Female sea turtles return to their natal beach to lay clutches of eggs, sometimes crawling up onto that singular stretch of sand forty years after leaving it as a hatchling. Turtles who may have wandered a thousand miles across the ocean somehow find the way back, like salmon with hundred-pound shells. Scientists think that they navigate by an internal magnetic compass. Or by smell. Or by the stars.

There's a variety of opinion.

A male sea turtle, on the other hand, stays at sea for life. Nature intends that he cross the beach exactly once, at birth. After mating at sea, the female goes off to find her special beach while the barnacle-encrusted, knot-headed old male spends the rest of his days adrift, eating, drinking, and waiting to mate again. He's got no compass, no ultra-sensitive olfaction, no celestial navigation.

I kept on course until my glowing depthfinder showed fifty-five feet and the GPS navigation display showed my latitude as 34-30-and-something North, longitude 76-30-and-change West. Beginnings are arbitrary, and Ilse and I had picked that spot simply because it's where the three-mile limit abruptly stops running parallel to the coast. At that point the line bumps out, further offshore, to make room for the Cape Lookout Shoals. Ilse and I had a history with those shoals, and the limits of international waters.

Feathering the crane controls, I eased the turtle over the side. When I released the sling he swam away strongly, then surfaced once, just off the stern. That turtle could have been a hundred and fifty years old. Older than the lighthouse. Older than Detroit Diesels, Jacuzzis, and JungleGolf put together.

Old enough, I thought, to know better.

chapter two

Spring turned to summer, and as the shrimping season began in earnest the Croaker Neck harbor warmed into its busiest season of the year. One morning, after an utterly routine turtle rescue I was tying up my slip when I saw my old friend Johnny Bollard culling the night's catch on the stern of his trawler, the *Lady Ann*.

"That might go faster if you had an even number of fingers," I needled.

He was too busy to be screwing around with the likes of me. Even with nine digits his hands were a blur as he sorted out the thirty-count shrimp from the jumbos that could go fifteen to the pound. His thickly muscled hands moved rapidly over the culling tray like a Vegas card dealer's, tossing the shrimp into coolers and the bycatch, mostly tiny fish, over the stern, where a flotilla of pelicans waited.

"Mind your lines, Dodge," he said. "And save the jokes for the dingbatters." A dingbatter is the local term for a tourist, or any other person who's from *off*.

Heeding Johnny, I threw another half-hitch around the piling. This turtle run had been nothing special—a loggerhead had been found floating near the inlet by some flounder giggers. He'd only been stunned, probably from being hit by a propeller. The old boy was tough, and when Ilse pronounced him well enough to swim I'd taken him to the secret spot near the shoals and released him. I hadn't encountered Agent Gatlin and his accusatory stare.

As my night's voyage had completed its long circle back to Croaker Neck harbor Johnny and the other shrimpers had just come in from a night dragging their nets through the sound. Meanwhile, fishing boats heading out for the day were tied up at Fowler's fish house, where the captains and hands were stooped over wide shovels, loading crushed ice into their holds. The men worked steadily, tending to their chores quietly, the way tired men do. Those who had been out all night were weary for sleep, those getting ready to go were weary from waking up far too early for too many mornings.

Locked in its busy silences, the Croaker Neck harbor would never be confused with a marina or a yacht club. Narrow and decidedly unimproved, it is a harbor of refuge. What the old timers call a hurricane hole. Protected by the Banks to the east and south, and most of North America at the remaining quadrants of the compass, it offers protection from all but the worst imaginable storms. Every vessel in the harbor belongs to a family of this town, and each slip—a rectangle of water with a piling at the corners—is passed along as a legacy. There is no dock space for rent here, no weatherproof power outlets or novelty doormats stitched with "Welcome Aboard," no golf carts to ferry gear or a yachtsman in a hurry. The pilings are replaced and bulkheads repaired without a lot of attention to the complicated government permitting processes. For their own projects, developers and second homeowners always hire enviro-lawyers and follow the rules to the letter, mainly because they've got a lot to lose. The fisherman in Croaker Neck harbor bends those rules for an even better reason, something more valuable than a slip that has no legal title anyway. What he stands to lose is just this: the way it's always been done.

Like Johnny's *Lady Ann*, named for his wife, most of the boats in the harbor bear the names of women: *Miss Susan* and *Janey L.*, *Sally Jean* and *Mary Rose*. They are "called after" wives and mothers, daughters and favorite aunts. The names are intended to honor the women ashore and bring luck and safety to the men at sea. And to make more of those men, you'd never find a better mold than Johnny Bollard, whose stout chest and bowed legs are the perfect combination for life on a rolling deck. His thick forearms and hands are tanned like cowhide, and so is his face, all except for the reverse raccoon-eye circles where his sunglasses cast their shadows. The skin on the bridge of his nose is pink and looks nearly worn through, like the knee of his yellow oilskin bibs. Johnny's intensity at his work, the black T-shirt under the bibs and a yellow-and-black Cat Marine Engines hat pulled low over his eyes, made me think of a buzzing yellowjacket all wound up and ready to sting.

"I see you been out with your turtle ambulance again," he finally said.

"Got to make a living."

"Where was this one?"

"Up near the beach."

"Not soaking in a hot tub, huh?" Neither Ilse or Agent Gatlin would have been pleased, but everyone in Croaker Neck had gotten a good laugh out of the loggerhead in the Jacuzzi.

"I guess you never know where these endangered species are likely to turn up, do you?"

"Threatened species."

"Well, whatever. Must be good for your business, though."

"I think I like it better when the turtle strands itself. Loses his way on the beach and that sort of natural stuff."

"Who's to say the turtle didn't crawl into that hot tub on his own? Just to unwind."

"It's not so funny," I warned him. "They've got some new kind of cop over there on the beach, a Fisheries special agent."

"He's not going to bother me," Johnny said. "I haven't so much as touched a turtle in three years. I've got turtle shooters on every net I own."

"Turtle shooter" is the local name for a *Turtle Excluder Device, or TED*—a hatchdoor placed in a trawler net that lets sea turtles escape. The turtle backers think that the holes aren't big enough to let adult turtles get free. The shrimpers think they're too big and let out too many shrimp. They say that TED really means "trawler elimination device."

"You see the head turtle kisser tonight?" Johnny used another one of Ilse Brunner's nicknames, and a very tame one. He avoided using the worst of them because he liked to be known as a church-going man.

"She's always spoken kindly of you," I said.

"Actions speak louder, bud. Isn't she throwing in with Gus Ridge?"

"Not that I heard about," I answered, not quite honestly.

In the newspapers, Gus Ridge is usually referred to as "a Raleigh businessman and conservationist," but in Croaker Neck he's better known as a country-clubber who bought his way into success as a tournament fisherman. A top-five finisher in the Pro Division of the king mackerel circuit four years in a row, he still had time in his schedule to become president of the Suburban Conservation Council. As head of the SCC, Ridge rode into town like Wyatt Earp on a 600-horsepower white Reggie Fountain powerboat, declaring that he was going to tame the cowboys and clean things up for the decent people. He claimed that new laws were needed, otherwise desperadoes like Johnny Bollard would net the fish and shrimp to extinction. But in ten years of trying, even a group as well-connected as the SCC couldn't get its agenda through the state legislature.

Lately Ridge and the SCC had switched their efforts to the federal courts. With a newfound love for sea turtles, the king mackerel fisherman had his lawyers boning up on the Endangered Species Act, with the idea that they might sue to force the government to shut down shrimping and even flounder netting in turtle habitat. Part of their strategy was to get in bed with Tortugas Now!, which in Johnny's eyes could turn Ilse from being a harmless do-gooder into a genuine enemy. If the SCC could get traction in federal court, Ridge might end up with not just the Tortugans, but the National Wildlife Service, the National Park Service, and a half dozen other government agencies on his side.

On their side, Johnny and the rest of the saltwater cowboys had dwindling clout with the new breed of politicians, who saw fish-fry rallies and oyster-roast fundraisers as quaint relics of elections past. More regulations, farm-raised fish, and cheap imported seafood had everyone feeling boxed in. Commercial fishermen had always grumbled, but lately they'd gotten more agitated than ever. They had formed an organization, the Croaker Neck Seafood League, and rumors were flying about what they were up to behind the scenes. Something big was brewing, everyone said. But their problem was that homegrown or not, the Seafood League was working hard to do the impossible—organize the most independent bunch of ornery individuals left on the planet.

"You ought to tell Ilse to stay away from Ridge," Johnny said, climbing from the *Lady Ann* onto the dock. "You give your girlfriend that advice, Dodge."

"She's not my girlfriend."

"She still keeps you up nights, don't she?" He was grinning at me now. Johnny never could stay mad at the world for more than ten minutes. "You remember how I warned you about her? What I told you about not gettin' above your raisin'?"

"And I told you that's all over. The turtle business is just a job. Ilse's just a woman who signs my checks."

"Argghhhhh," he growled, heading off toward Fowler's fish house, striding down the uneven dock in his white plastic boots, the style they call Wanchese Wingtips.

The fish house is the commercial and social center of Croaker Neck, the place where fishermen and shrimpers take their catch to be weighed, packed in ice, and shipped. It's little more than a shack built out over the water with a dock out back and a driveway of shell leading to the tailgate-high loading dock. But in the season thousands of dollars in cash can change hands there every day as boxes of seafood are shipped out in refrigerator trucks bound for restaurants and markets in a dozen states. Not long ago the North Carolina sounds were ringed by scores of small local fish houses. Now there are probably more of them abandoned than working. The big operators have gotten bigger, while the small places sit and rot, waiting for the day they'll be torn down to create more waterfront lots.

But Fowler's is still alive, still pretty much the same as it was on that fall day when I first met Ilse there. Johnny was at the fish house that day, too.

It was a year without hurricanes, so the *Gannet* and I hadn't made much money pulling docks out of the sound. But the lack of storms meant the fish house was busy, so I could pick up some extra cash working there before the winter set in. I was shoveling ice for Dan Fowler's wife, Peggy, who was dressed out in a rubber apron and white boots, using a garden hose to de-slime a load of mullet before she lifted them one by one into a metal basket hanging from the scale. So I happened to be there a shovel in my hand, when the strange woman appeared in the doorway, backlit and blinking as her eyes tried to adjust from the bright sunlight to the cool darkness inside. She stood tall, dressed much better than any tourist I'd ever seen. The black leather coat she wore hung down below her knees, and the collar looked to me like it might be real fur. Her hair was shiny and red, a real deep red like old blood. Her age was hard to tell; a little older than me, maybe, but not enough to matter. I planted my shovel in the pile of white slush at my feet and went over to try and help this stranded, exotic creature.

"You need directions, ma'am?" Her eyes darted around the room, trying to take in everything at once. Up close, I could see the lines around those eyes. Hers was an uptown face, for sure—but not one that had been kept indoors.

"Thank you," she said, with an accent. She kept looking around, everywhere but at me.

"Vich fish are these?" she asked, nodding in the direction of the round fish that were hanging in a metal basket under the big spring scale. Maybe she was German.

"Those are jumping mullets," I explained.

"*Jumping* fish? Why does he *skveeze* the jumping fish?" the woman asked.

"To find the females," I said. "The eggs are very valuable."

"Is it . . . *caviar*?" she asked. Maybe she was Russian.

"Well," I shrugged, "down here we just call it roe."

We stood there and watched and I wondered at the familiar sensation I was starting to feel. Talking about fish sex had never done very much for me before. I snuck a glance at Dan Fowler, to see if he was catching any of this, but he was still busy sexing mullets. Peggy tried to keep her eyes on the scale. She and the foreign woman were nearly the same age, but Peggy had the build of a hard-working fishwife, including robust arms that didn't strain when she tipped the metal basket and fifty pounds of roe mullet spilled into a waxed cardboard box on the floor.

"What are those coppery fish with the spotted tails?" The redhead pointed at a smaller pile of fish over against the wall.

"We call those puppy drum."

"*Puppies*?" She laughed again. A sugary laugh, sweetened no doubt by its passing through those lips. She walked outside and I followed.

"Ma'am," I started, "if you need directions . . ."

"My uncle was a fisherman," she said a little dreamily. "Many years ago. In Lubeck." On my blank look, she said, "On the Baltic Sea. In Germany."

"Where is it you're trying to go?" I asked.

"Are they selling them?" She said, ignoring my question. "The puppy fish?"

She reached into the pocket of her leather coat and pulled

out a roll as big around as a full-grown mullet, peeled off a twenty, and handed it to me. I noticed there was a gold ring on the hand that held the roll, with another on top of it, silver with a big red stone.

"Go buy me a fish—" She paused, and made a tiny, subtle tilt with her chin. An impatient gesture, a demand, an invitation, all at the same time. Above the tilted chin she parted those lips. Lips that could talk you into writing a bad check. Or buying a fish.

"Dodge," I said. "My name's Dodge Lawson."

"I am Ilse." She handed me the twenty and went back to watching, and living in her universe, which harbored not even the slightest possibility that I would fail to do what she asked. I walked over to Dan Fowler and told him the red-headed tourist wanted to pay him twenty bucks for a fish.

"You doin' retail on your own now, Dodge? Cause I thought you were shovelin' ice for me."

"Old Red there gets done with Dodge, you'll be shovelin' his sorry ass off the floor," said Peggy, talking out of the corner of her mouth.

"Look, just sell the lady one of these drum."

Dan grabbed the twenty out of my hand.

"Does she want it dressed?" he asked.

"Whole," I said. "I can gut the damn thing, if that's what she wants."

"Dodge here's fixin' to take the day off." Peggy again.

"He's not going anywhere," said Dan.

"You wanna bet?" Johnny Bollard had been watching the whole thing from the dock, and now he couldn't resist joining in.

"What in the hell is so damn funny to you-all?" I'd lost any shred of cool, and it was so obvious that even hard-hearted Peggy was embarrassed for me. She went back to weighing fish, Dan went back to *skveezing*, and Johnny disappeared onto the dock.

I picked the biggest of the puppy drum off the floor and walked outside where the woman was leaned over inside her shiny new Lincoln. From inside the car she produced a folded brochure put out by one of the ferry services on Harkers Island.

"I want to see the Cape Look Out," she said.

"I've been trying to tell you . . . you missed the turn that takes you to the ferry. It's a few miles back."

"Won't you take me?"

"To the ferry?"

"It's getting late. Maybe you could take me to the Cape Look Out, instead." It wasn't a question.

"You can only get there by boat." I pointed through the fish house and across the sound, in the general direction of the cape. I also pointed right at Peggy, Johnny, and Dan Fowler, who were standing on the dock behind the fish house.

"Don't you have a boat, Mr. Lawson?" she asked. In fact I did, and it was tied up not thirty yards from where we stood. "I've come a very long way," she said. "And I'll pay you."

I looked up at the sky, then into the fish house, and finally at her. The sky was blue, the fish house was dark. She was beautiful.

"I guess it's a nice day for a boat ride."

Over on the dock Johnny tilted his cap back and grinned at me while Dan Fowler slipped some money into his hand.

I guess you could say that my love for Ilse started with a wrong turn. Or some idle chatter about fish roe. Or the fact that Johnny Bollard never loses a bet. Whatever the cause, I was caught. And unlike our town's namesake fish, I didn't have the good sense to let out even a croak in my own defense.

chapter three

Nearly two years later I was still enmeshed in Ilse's net, even though our only remaining contact was the turtle rescue business. The opportunity to stay in touch with her may have been my main reason for taking the turtle job, but it was far from the only one. There was the money I earned, and the excuse it provided to get out on the water or to hang around the harbor talking to Johnny and the other pros. I counted most of them as acquaintances and some as friends, including the salty old fisherman who called out to me just as Johnny was disappearing into the fish house door.

"Hey buddy!"

A wild shock of weather-styled wiry blond hair rose above the bushes and in the gathering light of day I could make out the disheveled form of old Pogy, standing next to the rickety dock that served as his home port. There's a boat captain's saying, "If you ain't been aground, you ain't been around," and Pogy had definitely been around. When fishing failed him, or his boat wouldn't run, he earned money by doing odd jobs around Croaker Neck. Then, with a little spending money in his pocket, Pogy was apt to run hard aground. But he would always get back to fishing at his earliest opportunity.

Which looked like his plan for today. He stood above his ditch with both bare feet on the gunwale of a peeling wooden skiff, trying to wrestle a pile of net off the dock. The boat could have made a good dinghy for a garbage scow, but it served Pogy's purposes. With a name that rhymes with Bogie, on a good day, in the right sort of light, Pogy might pass for Bogart's gin-drinking Mr. Allnut in *The African Queen*. But he actually got his name from a fish, the Atlantic menhaden, aka, the Pogy. Also known as bunker, shad, and fatback, the menhaden is a slab of oily flesh that runs in schools numbering in the millions. Fed on by everything from flounder to tuna, it's probably the Atlantic Ocean's one indispensable fish.

"Hey buddy," he yelled again, not noticing that I was standing right next to him.

"I'm right here, Pogy."

He squinted at my face and seemed surprised to recognize it.

"Roger-Dodger?"

"It's just plain Dodge. And you know it."

The golf shirt Pogy wore must have come from some dingbatter's cast-off wardrobe, the solid red faded to a threadbare pink. A darker spot on the left breast showed where the little polo player had fallen off. A section of dock line was threaded through the belt loops of his blue Dickeys work pants and knotted in a sheet bend just below the belly button. He wore a loop of Dacron fishing line around his neck, and on it were threaded odd bits of shell, a blackened shark's tooth or two, and other objects too obscure for description. The collection seemed to grow every time I saw him, and the weird necklace, along with his dark, weather-hardened skin and wild hairdo, gave Pogy the look of a Polynesian cannibal.

"Whatever you say, Roger-Dodger," he sing-songed. Pogy still liked to needle me with the obnoxious nickname he had stuck on me back when I was the Professor's kid hanging around the harbor wearing cut-off jeans and rubber flip-flops from the Kerr Drug. I never cared much for my high-sounding given name, Roger Dodge Lawson, and I really hated the corruption "Roger-Dodger." When I finally got the chance the first thing I did was become just plain Dodge.

"My net's hung up," Pogy said. "Help me out?" Irritated or not, I had to do it. Using a foot and both hands I managed to untangle the monofilament mesh, which itself was a perfect reflection of Pogy's scavenging ways. No two floats on the top line were the same. Over time they had been replaced with scuffed pieces of cork and plastic that had been carried on some random tide into his fluctuating inventory of spare parts. Here and there he had mended the net with different colored pieces of fishing line, and the knotted sections of blue, green, and fluorescent yellow made the mesh blanket one of a kind. Pogy's net was a patchwork quilt that, in his hands, at least, could catch a man's dinner or enough roe mullet to pay for gas and beer.

Once the net was shipped, Pogy untied his rope belt, wrapped it around the starter pulley on his outboard motor, and yanked the machine to life. It might have been an Evinrude or a Johnson; the brand name was long gone, along with the cowling. Practiced hands swiftly re-threaded the double-duty belt, tying the sheet bend in a single motion. He stood there squinting up at me, his head cocked to one side, like he was listening to something I couldn't hear.

"According to the Bible," Pogy said, snatching the reference out of nowhere, "the whale was the first living creature, and the largest that God ever created. He put 365 bones in its mouth for the days of the year. And He gave man dominion over it. That's Genesis 1:21," he concluded, looking up at me with a smile that showed about an equal number of gaps and tobacco-stained teeth.

Nodding at me, Pogy settled onto the skiff's aft bench and turned the throttle on his tiller. The boat whipped around in the harbor and out into Ballast Creek. A blue heron flushed at the noise, and I saw the great bird suspended above Pogy, both of them silhouetted against the marsh as it held the soft morning light like milk in a saucer.

At the other end of the harbor I could hear another boat was leaving port, a gray fiberglass skiff much larger than Pogy's, with twin outboard motors big enough to push a load of two survey crews and all their gear. The surveyors had been going off to work like that every morning for a week, headed for Murdock's Island, the hundred acres of woods and marsh that lay just across from the mouth of Ballast Creek. With their theodolites and laser beams they were carving up the last sizeable chunk of uninhabited private land in Core Sound. A Florida developer named Oscar Cruz had big plans that would turn Murdock's Island into a pricey condo development with boat slips all around. This invasion from *off* was not real popular in Croaker Neck, and the night after Oscar's workmen planted his real estate sign out next to the highway, someone had driven a truck over it. But underneath the tire tracks you could still read, "Cape Lookout Condominiums—A True Sportsman's Paradise. Starting at $299,000."

Were he still alive, my grandfather would have bought a drink for whoever ran down the realtor's sign. Granddad liked Croaker Neck just the way it was when he first discovered it, after his irrepressible curiosity inspired him to leave a cozy classroom at the university and head off to risk everything testing his ideas about barrier islands. One day he tossed a canvas bag of geologist's tools and sample jars into his old Chevy Suburban and started driving east. Eventually he found himself at the harbor, where he asked one of the old salts if he could rent a boat to go to the Banks on university business.

"No boats for rent that I know of," the man said. "But I'll carry you yonder to the Banks, if that's where the university wants you want to go." The old salt was Johnny Bollard's father, a boat builder and mullet fisherman everyone called Big John. That day, as they motored across Core Sound, Granddad told him what he thought he might be looking for. Away from the campus, looking at the vast stretch of water and the endless line of dunes on the eastern horizon, he had the frightening revelation that his theories were all guesswork. But Big John was listening, and when they got to the far side he piloted his wooden skiff into the mouth of a hidden marsh creek that ended in a teacup of a bay unmarked on any chart. Leaving the boat at anchor, the two of them walked across to the beach side.

"Let's wait here," Big John said, taking a seat on a block of driftwood and pulling out his pipe.

"Wait for what?" asked Granddad.

"Low tide"

The mysterious ways of his clamp-mouthed guide weren't

doing anything to help his anxiety, so he found his own driftwood seat and pulled out the bottle of bourbon that he always kept in the bag with his tools. As the tide ebbed, the two men passed the bottle. Two hours passed, and then Granddad watched in wonder as the receding surf uncovered the peaty remains of an ancient maritime forest. Tree stumps, blackened by time, stuck up improbably in the white ocean foam. Big John smiled around his pipe, tickled by the sight of the big university professor dancing through the surf and taking samples of the peat sands as he went. The bourbon bottle was empty when they got back to Croaker Neck harbor that day, because Granddad knew that those fossilized stumps had only one explanation— that the Banks *were* turning over, that today's beach had been soundfront property long ago. And he could prove it!

After that day Big John Bollard made better wages than any fisherman in Croaker Neck, as an unofficial employee of the university geology department. Soon his son Johnny was on the payroll, too, earning himself a dollar every time he carried the canvas bag of tools and necessities across the Banks.

Granddad bought a little place just across Ballast Creek from the harbor. He called it the Down East Environmental Project, or DEEP, which was a pretty fancy name for a three-room cabin with a screen porch and rotten boat dock. That cabin became his refuge from the university town up on the hill. He'd take me off to the DEEP cabin whenever he could, often over the loud protests of my mother (his daughter) who had married one of the big-time doctors at the medical center. She thought I ought to be taking tennis lessons, or going to classes in comportment.

The boat that Big John Bollard used to carry Granddad and his tools across the sound was a juniper pole skiff he built with his own hands. Big John's hands were fluent in his craft, and the skiff trimmed out perfectly when the load was two adults and two boys eager to spend another day horsing around on the Banks. Those were by far the best days of my childhood: Granddad digging in the sand and then writing in his notebook; Big John sitting on the gunwale of the beached skiff, puffing his pipe; Johnny and I using a cast net to catch finger mullets on the flats, or sneaking through the sea oats to throw shells at sitting gulls.

Even though he was a little younger, it was Johnny the men first trusted to handle the skiff on his own. We started to make our own voyages out on Core Sound, to set a net and drink beers that I'd stolen out of Granddad's cooler. Johnny liked to smoke, too—Kools, of all things.

In the morning we'd go back and pull the net, and in my memory, at least, it beats any Christmas I can recall. We'd snag the end of our net with a short-handled gaff and start pulling until a treasure chest of fish would come wiggling over the transom. Our booty would include croakers, bluefish, spots, trout, and once in a while a coppery puppy drum. But the best catch was roe mullet. We'd hurry them back to the cabin on Ballast Creek, where Granddad would fry the roe sacks in bacon grease and serve them on top of scrambled eggs with the bacon crumbled over.

"Fish eggs and hen's eggs," he'd say, closing his eyes to chew. "True manna from heaven."

A university booster with ties made a grant to the DEEP project, which Granddad used to buy an old Core Sounder-style wooden boat. The donor also threw in enough cash to have the boat outfitted with a crane and a few pieces of electronic gear, making her suitable for research. A new coat of paint was applied, white with black trim.

"What'll we call her, Roger?" Granddad asked.

"How about the *Gannet*?" I said, thinking of the big black-and-white birds I'd seen dive-bombing bait on the Cape Lookout Shoals.

"*Gannet* she is," he said, drinking from the bottle of champagne that he couldn't stand to waste cracking across her bow.

Big John had pointed out the giant black-and-white birds one December day. I loved them for their snow-white downy bodies, the stark black wingtips, and the way they would fly high in tight formation and then peel off one by one to bombard a school of bait, tucking their wings in to hit the water at tremendous speed and just the perfect angle. Back home on the hill, I had happened across a photo in *National Geographic* that showed their nesting grounds, a rock island off the coast of Iceland.

The lure of that larger world, presented in pictures, finally tapped into the romantic in me, and my boyish attitudes toward Croaker Neck and fishing with Johnny Bollard began to change. It was Big John's plan that his son perform actual work, while I was free to play around most of the time. But even though Johnny had real work to do, when I was visiting he would make time for us to set nets and drink beer in the evening. Eventually, I was the one who strained our friendship, when I started to prefer catching fish with a hook and line. I might never have developed such a bad habit if I'd spent all my time in Croaker Neck; but for long stretches of the year I was stuck in cul-de-sac hell, living in the starter mansion my mother thought was barely large and pretentious enough for a surgeon and his wife. There I would sit in my bedroom, far from the water, reading and re-reading every issue of *Field & Stream*, especially the stories by Robert Ruark.

It was only a matter of time before my pseudo-sophistication took its toll. The summer I turned fifteen I showed up in Croaker Neck drunk on the idea that I, too, was a Sportsman. Another Ruark, Gowdy . . . even a Hemingway. Like my new heroes, I'd grown too worldly-wise to waste time pulling a gill net.

Youth may be wasted on the young, but stupidity sure isn't.

Not that my new scruples much mattered to Johnny Bollard. He was growing up for real instead of passing through the rites described in magazines, and already he was well down the road to the tough life of the saltwater cowboy. While I was watching TV he'd learned to haul a net full of gray trout, and how to tighten a purse seine around a school of shad. Big John taught him how to dip fish out of their pound net in the sound, and where to tong oysters on the rocks in Ballast Creek. By the time my parents sent me off to college in California, Johnny had already gotten an education and could earn his own living off the sounds and the sea. He got married and had two kids, and managed to keep a roof over their heads by commercial fishing.

While Johnny was becoming a saltwater cowboy, I was *off*, way *off*, first at college and then just knocking around out West. When I ran out of money I came back to Croaker Neck and moved into the cabin on Ballast Creek with Granddad, who still delighted in throwing a cast net off his dock for shrimp and mullet, and still jotted in his research notebooks every day. He had perfected the art of living simply, putting most of his state pension check in the bank and savoring the fresh seafood, ducks, and venison that friends and neighbors brought by, depending on the season. Even though I'd blown my college education, wasting a small fortune in the process, he was happy to support me until I could get on my feet. There was no indication he agreed with his daughter's opinion that her only son was a failure. But I couldn't shake my own feeling that her assessment was right on target.

The *Gannet*, retired from research and badly in need of repair, was tied up at the cabin's dock on Ballast Creek, where I kept her company, sitting in a lawn chair reading books chosen for their pointlessness.

"Maybe you could fix her up," Granddad said, trying to be helpful. "Get your captain's license and hire her out to the university again." When I told him I felt like I'd be a hazard to navigation, he just smiled a sad smile and walked away.

Like many a lost boy I stayed in that never-never land until events finally forced me to do some of the growing up that was so desperately overdue. Granddad turned eighty on the Fourth of July, and he consented to let me drive him to Chapel Hill for a celebration held in my mother's back yard. It was a swell affair, with catered food on silver trays, and she surprised him by tracking down and inviting the few of his university colleagues who were still above ground. The gesture was an unusually kind one for her, but the real motive became clear after the party, when she, backed up by my father, began to press Granddad to quit Ballast Creek and move into an assisted living facility near campus. Such a move was the farthest thing from his mind, but just the mentioning of it seemed to break his spirit. On the long drive back to Croaker Neck he was silent, and for the next two weeks I noticed him shuffling around the cabin in slow motion. Once I caught him standing out in the yard, just staring at the camellia bush that wouldn't bloom for another six months.

I happened to be out walking the day Granddad fell off his own dock. I came back to Ballast Creek around sunset and found him face down where his sweater had snagged on an old piling. The cheap Seiko tide watch that I'd bought him for his birthday was still on his wrist, showing the water as ebbing. A loose sleeve was all that had stayed the falling tide from carrying his body out into the sound.

Later, the doctor said he'd had a stroke, and assured me that he didn't suffer. My mother insisted on holding the funeral back in Chapel Hill, where she wouldn't have to share whatever grief she could muster with Granddad's true friends, the fishermen and crabbers.

It broke my heart to see his casket lowered into that soulless orange clay so far from the water, so when I got back to Croaker Neck I threw a proper wake at the cabin. Half the town turned out, many of them older people who'd known Granddad well but hadn't visited in years. Johnny Bollard came to the wake, too, and at midnight the two of us were standing out by the creek with a bottle of George Dickel.

"This was the Professor's brand," he said, swigging from the bottle. "I remember because it was the bottle that made that canvas bag of his so damned hard to carry."

"He thought a lot of you," I said. "And your daddy. You taught him how things work in this country."

"I'll tell *you* something—I learned things from your

Granddad, too. About this place, and how special it is. Without knowing him, I might be just like everybody else here. Taking things for granted."

"Remember when we used to set our own net out of that skiff your daddy built?"

"Sorry, but what I remember best about that boat is how it killed him." I was reminded of how Big John had died after he'd had such a good strike of mullet that the boat got too heavy and caught on the bar at the inlet. When it flipped in the surf, Big John got tangled in his own net and drowned.

"Funny thing," Johnny went on. "The year before he died, Daddy built a skiff that was twin to that one, down to every little detail. The Maritime Museum people in Beaufort wanted it for their collection. I've still got the damn thing, sittin' in the yard." He swigged from the Dickel and handed the bottle to me. Somewhere out in the creek a jumping mullet splashed down.

"I'm sorry they're both gone," I said.

"It's okay. Big John and the Professor are probably out yonder right now." He pointed toward the Banks and his reaching was immediately answered by the lighthouse at the cape winking at us from across the void of the sound. In that instant I was sure he was right, that if Heaven was of any use to us then it wasn't up in the sky but right out there where we could reach it in a small wooden boat.

I started re-fitting the *Gannet* the very next day.

Granddad's death jolted me out of my prolonged slack tide. Back in the world again, I noticed that Croaker Neck was changing. As the hard crabs died or went off to the rest home, dingbatters were buying up the old yellow-pine homes, paying good money to restore them and applying for their historical plaques before the paint was even dry. Once settled into their weekend retreats, they'd walk or ride their bicycles to the end of the road to view the quaint harbor with its shrimp boats and wooden pole skiffs. It didn't take them long to start feeling left out. Surely, for the right price, a slip might become available for their sportfishing boat or that small day-sailer.

If the Banks themselves couldn't stay in one place, what chance did one little town have? After we found the loggerhead in the Jacuzzi, events began to whirl like a hurricane, a storm whose outermost band of squalls came ashore in the form of a New York movie director who called himself Will Shutterspeed.

chaPter four

The first I heard of Will Shutterspeed was when Digger Davis came by the cabin on Ballast Creek to tell me there was a new dingbatter in town. I was down working on my dock when Digger pulled up in his beat-up blue Dodge Powerwagon, its back bumper decorated with the bumpersticker that reads, I LIKE TO SEE TURTLES SWIM, TOO . . . WITH TATERS AND ONIONS.

"Have you heard about the new dingbatter in town?" he asked excitedly.

Digger was in his usual clothes—deck shoes with no socks, many-pocketed canvas shorts, and a button-front shirt with a Guy Harvey blue marlin on the back. He keeps his hair cut short and a dome of broomstraw bristles was exposed through the visor-style cap that shaded his eyes but left his bleached crew cut and sunburnt scalp open to the weather. A pair of wraparound Costa del Mar sunglasses made Digger's face unreadable. He wore the fancy shades winter and summer, day and night. Like his attitude, his entire wardrobe was left over from his days as a Morehead City charterboat captain. When he first got to

Croaker Neck he was the best-dressed cowboy in town, but lately all of his stylish duds have gotten worn and nearly threadbare.

"In case you haven't noticed," I pointed out, "there's new dingbatters arriving every week."

"This one's different. He rented Clarence Rugby's old crab house, and he's gonna open up a movie studio. Clarence thinks maybe he's going to make porno films." The way Digger says *porn*-oh, it sounded extra dirty.

"Come on Dodge, let's go see," he needled. "It's just down at the end of the road." Digger's interruption had caused me to whack my thumb with the hammer, so out of a combination of frustration and curiosity I dropped my tool belt and climbed into his truck. On the way Digger had more news than just the movie director's arrival.

"Did you hear about the big demonstration the Seafood League is planning?" Digger shouted over Bob Seger singing about Hollywood Nights.

I had read about it. One day fliers had appeared in the harbor, green and yellow quick-printed pages calling for a "Rally in Raleigh" at which the citizenry would "Defend Your Right To Fish!" A flier was stapled to just about every piling, and the dock at Fowler's fish house was plastered with them.

"A demonstration, huh? You all going to hold hands and sing 'We Shall Over-fish?'"

"You might be surprised."

At the end of the paved road, near the water, we turned left onto two sandy ruts leading into a grove of pines. The low spots where a truck might get stuck had been partly filled in with crushed shells covered over in the really bad places by a layer of roofing shingles. The crab house squatted at the water's edge. Even in better times it had been nothing more than a flimsy building of rusty corrugated sheet metal set up on a concrete slab next to the water. Straddling the line between temporary and permanent, these metal structures are the standard quarters for commerce out here. They shelter everything from tire repair to barbershops to crab picking operations like the one Clarence Rugby used to run.

When Digger and I pulled into the crab house yard we were greeted by a pile of junk freshly heaped up outside the front door—a few broken-up plywood tables, half a dozen ruined wire crab pots, an old metal cooler, and bushels of empty beer cans and peeling bottles. Close by the junk pile roared the Briggs & Stratton engine of a high-powered pressure washer vibrating on its metal skids so violently it seemed in danger of shaking itself apart. A quivering length of black hose led into the open door of the steel building where it disappeared into a cloud of mist. Inside the jetted water rattling off the corrugated walls must have been deafening.

"See what I told you?" said Digger.

In the middle of the trashy yard sat a new-looking white Chevy van, the windowless commercial model. This one had New York plates.

We tried to stay off to the side of the doorway to keep away from the wet stuff billowing out. Around the corner of the building I could see a brand new diesel generator still shrink-wrapped to its pallet. It looked powerful enough to light the whole town.

While we stood there the washer motor began to cough, and after missing a couple of beats it quit altogether. The racket inside stopped, too, and we heard "What now?" shouted loud. Then came angry banging against the metal walls, as if there were some kind of caged beast in there trying to get out. Through a cloud of dirty steam lingering in the doorway stepped a big goggle-eyed fellow dressed in a suit of Carhartt overalls soaking wet from the knees down. He stopped to push the goggles back onto a head of hair that was as white as if it had been limed. The mane was long and bunched into a ponytail that crawled into hiding under the corduroy collar of the brown canvas overalls. The big man stood there sweating and blinking in the sunshine until he looked over and saw us standing next to the truck. His face was red; I couldn't say whether it was the flush of anger, exertion, or just the contrast with his white hair.

"Can I help you?" He sounded low on breath.

"Looks like it's you could use the help, cap'n," said Digger.

"I probably could," said the man as he walked over to look at his power cleaner. Then, as if remembering something, he turned and asked, "Who are you guys?" The goggles had slipped down over his forehead so that he seemed to have an extra set of bug eyes above his snowy eyebrows.

"Just the locals," Digger shrugged. Baiting the new guy a little.

"My name's Dodge Lawson," I said. "This is Digger Davis."

"Shutterspeed," he said, sticking out a big hand. "Will Shutterspeed."

"Welcome to Croaker Neck, Mr. Speed." Digger was being a wise ass, but the nickname he'd just coined would eventually stick.

Shutterspeed finally took the goggles off his forehead. He went 6'3" and 250 pounds at least, and looked younger than his white hair would make him. In the Carhartts he could have passed for a hippie welder, if he didn't look so clean. Even in the soaked coveralls Shutterspeed still projected good grooming.

"Looks like you've got big plans for Clarence's crab house,"

Digger began, starting what I recognized as a typically sideways Down East interrogation. People here are usually able to extract all the detailed information they need, even though it's considered impolite to ask any question more direct than, "How they bitin'?"

"I'm making a film," Shutterspeed confessed.

"Porno?" I asked.

"Not porno." The big guy scowled at me. "Not funny, either."

"Sorry. Bad joke."

"A man wouldn't come to Croaker Neck to make *porn*-oh," Digger agreed. "Women here's all Baptists."

The new guy laughed at that, but then turned serious again.

"I'm working to finish a documentary film."

"Like on public TV? The Civil War?" Digger had watched half the first episode before declaring it "Yankee bullshit."

"It's something like that."

"I s'pose Croaker Neck is as good a place as any for that kind of thing," Digger asked without asking.

"It's close to my subject matter," Speed explained. "The locations I'll need. And the rent is cheap."

"One thing we got here, it's subject matter," Digger agreed. "Yes, sirrrrr."

Shutterspeed could stand no more of this fooling around.

"Did you ever hear of the Lost Colony? Virginia Dare?"

"Sure. Everybody has." Every North Carolina public school student has, anyway. It's one of the first things you learn in your public school state history class. Downeasters have their own version, which Digger began to explain about. I'd heard the tale many times before and always considered it pretty goofy, but when Digger got to the part about the Coree tribe and their blond hair and blue eyes Shutterspeed surprised me by chiming in with something close to agreement.

"In 1709," he said, "the English explorer John Lawson reported seeing Outer Banks Indians with gray eyes."

"Maybe that Lawson was kin to you, Dodge." Digger pointed at me and proudly informed Shutterspeed, "His grand-daddy wrote books, you know."

"Really?" The way the big guy raised an eyebrow made me wonder if he was thinking *porn*-oh, too.

"My grandfather was a geologist."

"Oh."

"From the university," Digger added, finding the reaction unsatisfactory. For some reason many people are surprised to learn that I come from an educated family.

Changing the subject, Shutterspeed kicked at the pile of debris we'd been standing around, looked up and said, "Maybe you guys know how I can get rid of this junk."

"Might make a good artificial reef," Digger said.

"That's—" Shutterspeed broke off, and our eyes followed his to the door of the crab shack. From out of the dripping mess inside walked a thin, black-haired young woman who looked a little pale for our climate, and a bit over-dressed in khaki pants and a coral shirt with epaulets. She was attractive in that long-legged, high-built way, and just as I was thinking that maybe Shutterspeed had scored the Stanley Cup of trophy wives, he introduced the woman as his assistant.

"Melinda Helms," she said, holding out a bone-white hand.

"This is Dodge and Digger. Local fellows. Fishermen, I believe. I was trying to volunteer them to get rid of this mess."

"In that case, I'm *very* happy to meet you," she said. While I was still shaking her hand a mosquito landed on the back of it. She wrenched free and smacked it, but too late. A smear of blood and smashed wings marked the spot.

"What *do* you think?" Shutterspeed asked. "About the trash?"

"We're glad to help out," Digger said, aiming his grin at Melinda and gesturing in the direction of his Powerwagon, which held its usual load of torn net and old boat parts. "I need to go to the dump anyway. A little extra won't hurt."

Thanks to Melinda, Digger had dropped the redneck act in favor of minding of his manners. But then Shutterspeed forgot his own. Fishing a hand down inside his Carhartts and coming out with a wallet, he asked Digger, "How much do I owe you?"

"Forget it," Digger said so quick he stepped on the question.

"But—" Shutterspeed stopped when he saw Digger turn his back. I looked at the big guy, shook my head, and he put his money away. With a well-turned "Thanks!" the assistant went back inside while the three of us went to work loading the junk.

"I suppose all these old beer cans and bottles really should be recycled," Shutterspeed complained.

"Don't worry," Digger told him. "I'll separate it all when I get to the dump. Won't I, Dodge?"

"Yeah," I said. "Sure." Digger was scheming, but I wasn't sure what direction he was going until he volunteered to leave me behind.

"Dodge," he said, looking at me over the tops of his Costa del Mars, "I reckon I can handle the dump myself. I'm sure Mr. Speed has more chores he could use a hand with."

"You know anything about engines?" the big guy asked, nodding at the dead pressure washer.

"Oh, he's a regular Richard Petty." I knew the way Digger's mind worked, the schemes that hatched there like waterbugs. He wanted me to stay behind because, in his fantasy, I'd be snaking Melinda away by sundown at the latest. Knowing how miserable I was over Ilse, Digger was trying to set me up. Or at least inviting me to take the first shot. The underlying premise, a vestige from his charterboat captain days, was that Melinda would fall helplessly for *him* if he didn't get out of there right away.

Digger was full of crap, of course. But I stayed behind anyway.

With Digger and the load of junk on their way, Shutterspeed and I unloaded the Chevy van, which was packed with wooden crates and laundry hampers full of movie gear—assorted lights, cords, and odd sorts of rigging. We carried all that into the crab house, plus a number of hard-side cases of camera equipment. Most of the bigger cases had engraved metal tags identifying it as the property of a rental company in Long Island City, NY.

I broke a rolling sweat while we stacked it all in a clean corner that had been crudely walled off with sheets of plywood. Melinda was sweating, too, as she arranged the boxes. She had piled most of her jet-black hair on top of her head and pulled on a baseball cap over top of the pile. A few strands fell in front of her eyes when she turned her head, and she used delicate fingers to move them. Her blue-gray eyes sparkled like she'd waited all her life to make movies in a run-down crab shack past the outskirts of nowhere. In the heat Shutterspeed has gotten out of his overalls and was sporting a Hawaiian shirt and swimming trunks. Even though his white mane made it hard to judge his age, I estimated that Melinda was at least twenty years younger.

We all kept working steadily until finally, grabbing an unexpectedly heavy crate, I felt a twinge in my back and let loose a grunt.

"Are you all right?" Speed asked.

"Fine." But I'd had enough of being helpful in the cause of Digger's fantasy. When I found out the heavy crate was full of sandbags (for holding down the legs of light stands, Shutterspeed said), I decided I was wasting my time helping anyone fool enough to have hauled bags of rented *sand* from New York City.

Melinda came to the rescue with bottled water and three sandwiches made of Wonder bread stuffed with shrimp salad. Out behind the building a portion of Rugby's dock was still standing, and we sat down there and began to eat. "Local shrimp makes all the difference." Shutterspeed nodded as he spoke around a mouthful of sandwich.

Melinda thanked me for unloading the trailer. I waved away the thanks with, "I guess I'm just another Hollywood groupie," then nearly choked on the realization of how that might sound. But she was looking out toward the water, not really listening to me.

"It's an incredible view," Melinda said. "Don't you think?" I agreed with her, even though I'd been looking at it for most of my life. The sound was slick and the summer haze had yet to really take hold. I could easily make out a half-dozen pelicans flying low almost a quarter-mile away. In the shade of the dock a snowy egret was stalking a school of mullet minnows.

"So unspoiled," she added.

"The *touristas* will be spoiling it soon enough. A place like this is too nice not to be discovered." Shutterspeed's tone was that of a habitual contradictor.

"Are there many tourists here?" Melinda leaned in my direction again.

"They're coming. Right now, it's mostly sports fishermen who are buying second homes. The only real tourist attraction in town is listening to people talk funny."

"It's the accent I told you about," Shutterspeed explained. "*Hoi toiders.*" To me he added, "Melinda is an anthropologist by profession. Masters degree from Columbia University."

"Oh. Well, uh." I was stammering.

"Is that a bad thing?" she asked.

"No, not really. But we've had enough anthropologists come through this county to start a small college."

"Here?"

"Oh, yeah."

The rush of academics to our part of the world started when two linguistics professors from the state university went up to Ocracoke and spent a lot of time on screen porches, rocking and drinking iced tea with their tape recorders running. They wrote academic articles with titles like, "The Sociolinguistic Complexity of Quasi-Isolated Southern Coastal Communities," which I swear to you is a real title and not something I'm making up. Not long after that somebody discovered that the Core Sounders down here talk even funnier than an Ocracoker, and then came a full-on run of sociologists, socio-biologists, cultural anthropologists, and dialectologists.

People here do have their own way of talking. When you first hear them, they don't sound right. Or, *soand roight.* High tide comes out *hoi toide*, and when the wind drops and the water is flat, they say it's *slick cam.* Something that's screwed up is *mommicked.* Male blue crabs are *jimmies*, and a dark thundercloud is known as a *gillyard head.* Marsh has two meanings: soft ground, and the size of the holes (e.g., "two-inch *marsh*") in a net.

"But it's essential," Melinda said, "that these dialects be documented. Isolated populations are disappearing almost as fast as they're discovered. Soon everyone will sound alike."

"Killing off the indigenous people," Shutterspeed said.

I told him that Croaker Neck wasn't being killed off so much as crowded out.

"Are we part of the crowding?" Melinda was direct. And that wasn't the only way she made me think of Ilse.

"No, not at all. Your fixing up this broken down crab house is a fine thing. I was thinking more about the condo development on Murdock's Island." I pointed out over the sound, where one of the survey crews was working in plain view, hacking away at underbrush on the island.

"Why would anybody want to develop such a place?" Melinda sounded incredulous.

"The usual reason. Money."

"How will people get to it?"

"The plan is a water taxi, at first. But I'm guessing that eventually they would build a bridge. People who can afford to pay three hundred thousand bucks will have the clout to get a bridge built."

"Is this place so backward you don't have conservation groups?"

I decided to let Shutterspeed's "backward" comment go for the time being. "There's Tortugas Now!, but they're only interested in turtles. And the Suburban Conservation Council, but they're mainly big-time sports who need somewhere to keep their boats. SCC members are some of those lining up to buy the condos."

"Self interest," Shutterspeed grunted. "And not very enlightened."

"What about your friend? Digger?" Melinda leaned at me again. "What does he think about developing that beautiful island?"

"Nobody in town is too happy about it, unless his name is Murdock. But these people have been raised to believe in private property rights. As far as they're concerned, Old Man Murdock can sell his land to anyone he wants."

"What about you?"

"Dodge's father was a geologist," Shutterspeed misinformed her.

"That was my grandfather."

"But what do *you* do?" she asked. Melinda seemed very interested in my answer to her question, her sincerity somewhat exaggerated by the way she leaned forward in her chair to bring her face closer to mine. It was the gesture of a woman who was, or had been, self-conscious about being tall. When she was a teenager it probably telegraphed insecurity, but in a woman with features as composed as hers it came across as an attentive curiosity. With her pale skin, long body, and that intent look, she reminded me of that egret stalking the edge.

"I rescue sea turtles," I answered.

"Really?"

"Not long ago I found one in a Jacuzzi."

Just as I finished the story we heard Bob Seger through the pines and Digger pulled into the yard. Climbing onto the dock with a red box under his arm, Digger grinned and said, "Cold beer! Help yourself!" Melinda said "No thanks," and went back into the crab house, leaving Shutterspeed to drink beer with the boys.

"I really appreciate you helping me out," he said. "I have to admit I'm in over my head here."

I didn't say anything. Maybe Digger blinked behind his shades.

"What I'm getting at is that if you know anybody who could

use a little extra money, I'm looking for help. I've got to make this place livable, and after that I'll need to wall off the studio, put up the sound-proofing . . . . "

Handyman work made me think of Pogy and how much fun it would be to put the two of them together.

"Have you noticed a guy around town wearing a weird necklace?"

"Not that I remember."

"Well look for him, you'll see him. That's Pogy. He doesn't talk a lot, or make much sense when he does, but he's good with tools."

"Where can I find this Pogy?"

"We'll send him your way."

As we were leaving, Shutterspeed went back to cussing at his power washer. I wondered if he'd noticed his "assistant" flirting with me. I also wondered if she really had been flirting, or if Digger's fantasy was growing, kudzu-like, in my head.

The following week Pogy once again put his nets away and went to work in town. He could often be seen walking out of the minimart with a twelve-pack under each arm, his face wearing the happy expression of the casually employed. Going to the crab house that day had been Digger's idea, and for a long time I tried to convince myself that it was his idea to put Shutterspeed and Pogy together. But I always knew the truth. That I was to blame right from the beginning.

chapter five

The New York film director and his anthropologist assistant made an odd couple. Throw in the Croaker Neck shallow-water shaman and the scene around Rugby's crab house became odder still. But every time I stopped by progress was obviously being made. Tolerable housekeeping quarters had been set up in the end of the building nearest the sound, where a rectangular window gave an unobstructed water view. A set of walls freshly Sheetrocked and painted set this area off from the studio. I was impressed by how livable the place had been made, furnished as it was with a four-burner propane stove, a side-by-side refrigerator that dispensed ice through the freezer door, a fancy leather couch and, behind a folding bamboo screen, a king-sized bed. One wall was floor-to-ceiling corkboard, to which was push-pinned the NOAA charts covering the waters from Beaufort Inlet to Cape Henry in Virginia. Notes had been scribbled on the charts, and note-filled index cards were tacked around the margins, as high on the wall as the big man could reach.

Just as the crab house had changed, there was something

different about Pogy. He seemed more serious somehow. When the construction was done, and Shutterspeed began to actually work on his Virginia Dare movie, he kept Pogy on, teaching him how to build sets and stage lights and dozens of other little jobs that the old fisherman took an unpredictable delight in learning. He still went off in his boat on occasion to explore the Banks or find more trinkets to go on his magic necklace.

One evening Digger and I were sitting on my screen porch when we saw Pogy's skiff leaving the harbor with Shutterspeed in the bow.

"I think our movie dingbatter is going native on us," Digger said.

I told him that what I couldn't figure out was the change in Pogy. "He's been working steady right along."

"I'd say it's that tall drink o' water with the dark hair that keeps him around."

"Melinda?" It always boiled down to one thing with Digger. Or two, if you counted fishing. Not that I hadn't taken notice of her myself. I'd even entertained the idea of inviting her over on the pretense that my grandfather's old sea chest was full of research notes that might interest her. Then I realized that my head might be getting filled with the same fantastic notions that kept Digger's noggin scheming full time.

Digger was a good friend, and after Ilse left me we spent many afternoons together, adding to the pile of empties on my screen porch. But sharing in beery consolation was one thing—I didn't want Digger to start having an influence on my thinking, particularly about women.

Not that he didn't bring a certain amount of experience to the subject. I'd first laid eyes on him at a party in Beaufort, where Digger was holding onto two blondes and a bottle of champagne. His boat, the *Doffin Coffin*, had just won over $200,000 in the Big Rock Blue Marlin Tournament. I recognized his female fans as two of the chamois girls who make their living wiping down the sport's big boats. A good chamois girl can make $200 a day in tips; whether it's the thongs they wear or their skill at leaving teak spot-free is difficult to say.

Captain Davis's unusual nickname was handed down to him from his father, Digger Davis, Sr., who owned a funeral home. Digger Junior grew up in the business, starting out learning how to cram dress shoes onto stiff feet. He went on to perfect the mortuary arts of dressing cadavers and applying makeup to ghostly faces to achieve that "natural" look the grieving relatives always remark on. Embalming school completed his professional education, but by that time he'd found his true calling, and it wasn't the family business. All Digger Junior ever wanted to be was a charterboat captain.

"If I'm gonna be messin' with a dead body," he said, "I want it to be something I can eat, or hang on the wall."

He once told me how he used to sneak out of the house before dawn and ride his bike down to the docks to watch the captains and mates get their boats ready for the day's trip to the Gulf Stream. Digger loved seeing the captain climb the slippery, dew-covered silver rungs up to the flying bridge, where he would open the electronics box and crank the big diesel motors to life. To the skinny and awkward undertaker's boy the captain looked like a god outlined against the Isenglass spray curtains, his face inside the halo cast by the glowing instrument screens. The captain always stood above it all, and Digger loved the arrogance, the way the god on the flying bridge would ignore the hungover sports as they stumbled aboard looking about as seaworthy as sickly sheep.

The summer after high school Digger got a job mating on the *Annabelle Lee*. He worked days that started long before dawn and ended with fish- and boat-cleaning chores at dinnertime. He learned to rig a dead bait that would swim as naturally as the living fish, and how to latch onto leaders to hand-over-hand big wahoos and billfish to the back of the boat. All the while he studied for the Coast Guard captain's test and passed it on the first try. He ran the *Annabelle Lee* for a while, and then another boat that Mr. Poe owned down in Little River, South Carolina. While he was away his father was killed in a freak traffic accident involving his hearse and a cement truck. Digger came back to Morehead City and the Davis family business buried its own proprietor.

Before the sod on his daddy's grave had taken root Digger sold his share of the funeral home to his younger brother and got the down payment on a used fifty-two-foot Jarrett Bay sportfisherman, which he re-named the *Doffin Coffin*. The years of mating had callused his hands and put tough, stringy muscles on a six-foot frame that was no longer awkward. The pale, skinny undertaker's boy had grown into the tanned, curly-haired *Captain* Davis, an up-and-coming god of his own flying bridge.

Unfortunately the U.S. Coast Guard has one of the world's strictest drug policies, including random testing. The captain of the *Doffin Coffin* had always been lucky, but there's such a thing as the wrong kind of luck, especially if you "win" the testing lottery. Later Digger would claim that he was the victim of second-hand smoke at a party. But that didn't hold any water with the authorities. His license was suspended, pending a hearing, but he kept fishing, telling his mate, "I got a boat payment, you know."

It's a big ocean, but the waterfront is a tightly-knit place occupied by highly competitive men, and not all of them liked

Digger's style. Evidence that he continued fishing without a valid license was presented at his hearing, and what could have been just a twelve-month suspension turned into a permanent revocation. It didn't help when he called the administrative law judge "a self-righteous prick."

When the Coast Guard pulled his ticket, *Captain* Digger Davis was history. He sold his Jarrett Bay boat at a loss, and moved from a condo in Morehead City to a trailer in Croaker Neck. One of the chamois girls came out to live with him, but she didn't take well to life in a trailer with a man who worked nights and spent his days smoking the high-octane local pot they call Pocosin Poison. ("If they're going to ruin my life over this stuff, I may as well go along," was Digger's backwards reasoning.)

Soon enough the girl went back to Emerald Isle and Digger was just another lonesome saltwater cowboy. By shrimping and fishing in the season and working a series of part-time jobs that didn't require any drug testing, he scraped together enough money to buy a very used twenty-three-foot center console boat. It was barely big enough for offshore fishing—the only kind that interested Digger. Partly as a favor to me, Johnny arranged dock space at the harbor.

Every week of decent weather brought a new promise from Digger to take me out fishing, but then we'd get into something else and end up on the porch, adding to our pile of empties.

"I'm thinkin' about going into taxidermy," he said on one of those lost afternoons, sitting in Granddad's old porch rocker.

"You? Mounting fish for tourists?"

"I'd specialize in big game. If I can embalm a two hundred pound human and make up his face so even his mama says he never looked sweeter, stuffing a bear should be a piece of cake."

Finally, he called with a real offer to go after dolphin.

"They're stacked up like cord wood at the ninety-foot break," Digger claimed. We were to meet in the harbor before sunup.

I made some bologna sandwiches, sharpened my fillet knife, and had all my clothes laid out. After setting my alarm for 4:30 I was about to doze off when the phone rang. Ilse said a security guard had spotted a turtle in the fountain outside the Carrot Island Country Club.

I gave her the standard response no matter when she called: "I'll be there."

It's my job.

Once again my nighttime course took me around Radio Island and under the high bridge over the Intracoastal. My approach to the country club was made easy by its location on a point just north of Beaufort, with deepwater access off the waterway. The first of Oscar Cruz's gifts to Carteret County, the club is nowhere near the real Carrot Island—a skinny strip of marsh in the Rachel Carson National Wildlife Refuge. I'm not sure if Oscar picked the name as some kind of joke on the environmentalists, or if he was really that stupid.

The entrance into the country club's marina was marked by a fake lighthouse so cheesy that it had to be rebuilt after every gale. With any luck the next decent hurricane would wash the entire Pete Dye signature golf course out to sea, too.

Ilse met me at the dock, and she was twice as angry as she'd been earlier at the Binnacle Inn.

"This *sheiss* is not funny, Dodge," she said through gritted teeth. "Whoever's abusing these turtles is going to be in big trouble."

"She's right about that." Special Agent Gatlin walked out of the dark, where he had been lurking while I tied up the boat.

Over at the fountain two security guards were pointing at the turtle and laughing, but they stopped when Ilse and the agent walked up. The fountain, an enormous three-tiered concrete monstrosity, complete with naked cherubs, must have been modeled after something Oscar had seen in Las Vegas. Lit by enough candlepower for three lighthouses, it looked far more out of place than the green turtle basking in the lower-level pool. He floated serenely above a tile bottom strewn with pennies and quarters while a glimmering shower rained down out of a cherub's wiener.

"This," Ilse seethed, "is a travesty." The turtle looked at us with one of its bulging, sleepy eyes.

"At least he's not soup," Gatlin offered. The green turtle's shell was actually light brown, with large mottled blotches of darker brown.

"He's not green, either," I said.

"The name comes from the color of his subdermal fat," Gatlin explained. "That's what you see when the turtler cuts him open to get the *calipee* from the bones of the bottom shell. That's what they make the soup from, the *calipee.* Some people like it so much that the green turtle has been wiped out in Bermuda and the Caymans."

"What's that?" Ilse pointed at a dark circle on the back end of the turtle's shell, right at the edge. It looked like a spot to me, but Ilse leaned over and stuck her finger through the shell.

"It's not a spot, it's a hole. And I saw the same size hole in the loggerhead underneath the Binnacle Inn."

"Are you sure?" Gatlin had taken a small digital camera out of his coat pocket and was zooming in on the hole.

"I didn't think anything about it, then," said Ilse.

"Well, what is there to think about it now?" I asked.

"You're sure you saw a hole in the loggerhead?" Gatlin still sounded skeptical. "All sorts of things can wear on the margin of a turtle shell. Maybe he was captured as a young turtle, and escaped." Ilse started to argue, but got cut off. "It's late," he said, not unreasonably. "Let me find our security friends and we'll get this turtle back out to sea." Then he went off to track down the rent-a-cops.

"Dodge," Ilse insisted, "someone has drilled a hole in both these turtles."

"Why would anyone do that?" As inclined as I was to take Ilse's opinion over the square-rigged agent's, the whole idea sounded nutty to me. Was she suggesting there might be a diver out in the sound with an underwater Black and Decker?

It took some creative rigging and a back-straining lift with the help of the reluctant guards, but we eventually got the turtle on the *Gannet's* deck, ready for its journey back home. Ilse and I worked closely to move the turtle, close enough for me to notice that her hair had a slightly gray cast to it, the way it got before she would go apply another treatment of henna. I still had a jar of the red powder in my cabin, one of the many things she'd left behind and never come back for.

Gatlin came up to stand on the dock, looking straight down at where I was unkinking a length of cable.

"Lawson, you're all wrong about me." The guy looked imposing as hell, like your worst nightmare if he got in a situation to use his fists, or worse, that Glock on his belt.

"What do you mean?"

"You think I don't belong here. That I'm just some kind of quota-hire game warden who doesn't want to get mud on my shoes."

I honestly had no idea what to think, except to steer clear of the guy.

"Ever hear of C.I.D.?"

I'd heard of C.I.D. It stands for Criminal Investigation Division.

"Army?" I asked him.

"United States Marine Corps. I may be new in this town, but I know how to ask the right questions. For example, I can't quite believe it's just coincidence that these strange turtle strandings are going on while your commercial fishing buddies are planning their big Rally in Raleigh."

My hand slipped on the cable and the salt-ragged wire cut into my thumb. I cursed, and stuck it in my mouth to clean the blood off.

"Careful there, Lawson," Gatlin warned. "And I mean that advice in every way." He got down on one knee so we were almost face to face. "You and the redhead, you make a very cute couple. But if you want to stay in the turtle-hauling business, you might want to consider moving away from Croaker Neck."

Then he walked his government-issue walk back across the lawn to where his lethal-looking black Suburban with the tinted windows was parked. I watched the big NOAA on the back of his jacket until he was inside the vehicle. New on the job or not, he'd already picked up on the prevailing attitude toward Croaker Neck.

With the real cop gone the rent-a-cops went back to their rounds, which likely included a nap in the caddy shack. That left me in the *Gannet*, and Ilse kneeling where the agent had been to get one last look at the green turtle.

"Are you bleeding?" she said, her voice much easier than before. If she was actually in a sympathetic mood, I thought I might try and press that point.

"Why don't you come with me? Ride out to the cape with our friend?"

"I would probably get seasick," she answered, looking off toward the cheesy fake lighthouse blinking on its jetty.

"You never got seasick in your life. Your family's fishermen, remember?"

Without realizing it I started reaching for her hand. She jumped back like my arm was a snake.

"We must never do that again, Dodge."

"Why? You find another guy?"

"I'm over that now," she said. "All that."

"*Over* it? You're not *that* old, Ilse."

"*Ahs*-hole."

"I'm sorry. I just wanted a chance to talk to you, is all."

She walked away. There was nothing for me to do but cast off and backtrack my course to the inlet. The turtle wasn't much company, and I kept hearing Gatlin saying, "You make a cute couple." That was what Johnny had said so long ago, that day at the fish house when he won his bet and I took the strange tourist woman to the cape.

Ilse and I were leaving Croaker Neck harbor in the *Gannet* with a falling tide and maybe four hours of daylight left. She stood beside me in the cabin wearing her long leather coat and clutching an expensive-looking leather bag. Her twenty-dollar puppy drum was on ice in my Igloo cooler next to a bottle of wine that she'd produced from the big green Lincoln.

Out on Core Sound the southwest breeze was picking up a little. At intervals salt spray came over the bow and landed on my windshield. A single stuttering wiper blade kept my side, the starboard side, clear. The German woman stared through the streaking saltwater drops on her side as if she didn't see them.

As we rounded the corner toward Cape Lookout Bight, I hoped she was enjoying the show—the green-gold marsh grass, the white sand, and the lighthouse. The exaggerated contrast between a seamless blue sky and the black-and-white diamond pattern on the lighthouse made the round tower of bricks appear flat, a page in a life-size picture book. Ilse and I were kids in a toy boat as the wild ponies of Shackleford Banks grazed on spartina grass at the edge of a sandy bluff across the bight from the lighthouse. I steered us to a spot where we could look directly up at the chewing horses. We saw them shake their heads at us, their chestnut manes like short, thick sails in the breeze. I watched Ilse watching the horses, both of us totally captivated by what we saw. Those ponies weren't half as wild or exotic to me as the creature whose own red mane was flaring in the October sunlight.

"I have heard of these horses before," she said softly. "Do they really live here?" She sounded a bit skeptical.

We drifted a while, back towards the lighthouse, and I asked her if she wanted to get out and have a look.

"Can we go up?"

"No," I said. "It is *verboten.*"

She smiled at my attempted German.

"Where is Cape Look Out? It sticks into the ocean, yes?" I

took out a chart and showed Ilse the lighthouse and then Cape Point, that arrowhead of sand pointing due south into the shoals. On a calm day I could have run out Barden's Inlet and around to the cape in thirty minutes. But with a gusty southwester blowing, the ocean would be no place for my *Gannet.* I explained all this to Ilse, but she wanted to go anyway.

"I must get there," she insisted. "I told you I would pay."

"Look," I said, "I'd give anything not to disappoint you. But I won't take this boat around that corner for all the money in the world." She said something in German. She actually stamped her foot. Then, she pouted those lips.

I looked at my tide watch, looked up at the sun, trying to judge how much water and daylight we might have left.

"I guess we could walk across the bank, if you want."

"I do want." She sat down on the engine cover, facing forward with an expectation to go, and go *now*. I put the transmission in gear, headed for the southeast corner of the bight where the government maintains a dock.

As we got secured she surprised me by dropping her attitude and helping with the lines. She lassoed a piling quickly, her feet steady on the dock, her cleating off as good as mine. This was a woman who'd spent time around boats. I handed up her leather bag, then transferred a flashlight into my slicker pocket along with the ignition key.

"Dodge?" she called from the dock. "Don't forget the wine."

We wound through the creases between the dunes until we came to the last high pile of sand between us and the ocean. When I got to the top I had to kneel in the sea oats and reach back for Ilse. Grasping my extended hand, she came up in two long strides. Finally seeing the ocean, she brought both hands to her face and peered through her fingers like a child.

"It is so beautiful!" She took it in for a moment, but then, back to business, she asked, "Which way is Cape Lookout?"

"You're standing on the cape right now."

She breathed in deeply as if she were trying to inhale more than just the salt air. "We must celebrate with the wine." Sitting down among the sea oats, she looked up at me with a worried look. "Do we have an opener?"

I fished in my pocket for the key chain I'd snatched out of the ignition. Like all prudent mariners, I've always kept my keys attached to a big floating fob; and, because I'm an extra-prudent mariner, there's also a Swiss Army Knife on the float. I flicked out the corkscrew and had the cork pulled before you could say *gezunheit*. We took turns drinking out of the bottle. We watched a pod of porpoises rolling in the whitecaps beyond the surf line. Ilse took it all in with approval, until she noticed the square-edged concrete foundations a short distance down the beach.

"What are those?" Each gray slab was the size of two railroad cars. Too big to ignore.

"Those are the gun mounts."

"Gun mounts?"

"Artillery pieces used to be mounted here, way back when."

"Way back, *when*?"

"Nineteen forty-two."

"These artilleries? Were they meant to kill Germans?"

"You . . . they . . . *were* the enemy, you know. Besides," I added, letting the wine do its talking, "in these waters it was the Germans doing most of the killing. With torpedoes."

We must have made a cute couple, all right, sitting there on that peaceful, romantic beach talking about artillery and torpedoes and who'd been killing whom. Now here I was, alone on the ocean in the dead of night, and the memory of that day sent a chill through me. Standing at the *Gannet's* helm I said, out loud, that I'd better get a grip. Nobody but the green turtle on my deck was there to hear me.

chapter six

After releasing the turtle I made my way back to Croaker Neck, pulling into the harbor just as the sun was coming up. My plan to go fishing was the farthest thing from my worn-out mind, but there was Digger, waiting for me. He laughed about the turtle in the fountain.

"Springtime, it was a Jacuzzi," he said. "Are you sure you're not just dreaming this stuff?" I told him I wished I was.

He looked around the dark harbor distractedly. "Keep an eye out for Pogy, will you?"

"Why's that?"

"He's going fishing with us." I told him I'd been up all night, complaining mightily, but it was no use. "You can sleep when the fish move on," he said. I was too tired to argue.

"Besides," he said, "I've got something I want to show you." That figured—nothing was ever Point A to Point B with Digger. We got the *Gannet* tied up and then walked down to where his twenty-three-foot center console Parker was warming up. It was no Jarrett Bay sportsfisherman, but with its T-top over the console and a fish box built into the transom, it would get the job done—as long as the seas weren't too rough. In the electronics box a VHF radio was crackling static so I punched the WX button for the NOAA weather forecast. Southwest winds ten-to-fifteen knots, waves two-to-four feet. A chance of isolated showers in the late afternoon. No worries there—just a typical day, made for fishing.

As the robot voice on the radio was getting to the extended marine forecast Pogy's mold-tinted shoes landed on deck. "Hey, Roger-Dodger," he greeted me, as Digger backed us out of the slip.

We passed the green marker at the harbor entrance and Digger put the hammer down. As the Yamaha's prop dug in, the Parker's big V nose rose up like a bucking horse, then quickly dropped down as the hull planed across the slick water of the sound. Day was breaking above the Banks, and the orange ball of the sun winked at me from just under the stainless steel bow rail. As usual the winds were calm but we were making our own, of twenty-five knots or so, and I turned the bill of my cap around backwards and faced into it. I was awake again and happy that I hadn't gone to bed. With my left hand I reached up to hang onto the rail of the T-top. The right I flung out to flap in the breeze like a flag, saluting one of the best ways I know to start off a day.

Beside me Pogy leaned into the wind and grinned his gap-toothed grin. The string of junk hanging around his neck seemed to have grown since the last time I'd seen him.

"What's that?" I asked him, fingering an oddly-shaped trinket that was dark on one side and bone color on the other. "Is that supposed to be good luck?"

"Arghh, for sure."

Instead of going out to the ocean, Digger made a left turn

and headed northeast up Core Sound. I stuck my head into the lee of the T-top and yelled in his ear, "Where are we headed?"

"I want to take a ride up yonder," he said. "Up the Indian ditch, to a place that Pogy showed me." I knew of at least three different so-called Indian ditches, but "up yonder" probably meant the Pamlico, so that narrowed it down.

"What're we doing there?"

"Just hang on, you'll see."

At Nelson's Bay he turned left, then idled under the big highway bridge and up the entrance to a curving alley of salt water that disappeared into the piney woods. Nature originally designed the creek as a dead end, but thirty years ago it had been extended as a six-foot-deep canal. There are several of these "Indian ditches." Maybe they were started by actual Indians, but most were made navigable in modern times by commercial fishermen with a notion to improve on geography. They saw that if they could connect this north-pointing creek here with that south-pointing creek up there, they could create a great shortcut between the sounds. The excavators used simple equipment, like a one-yard drag line, relying on singled-minded brute strength instead of technology.

The ditch Digger chose that morning is barely a boat-beam wide, walled in on either side by dense, swampy jungle. I was looking for snakes in the trees and he was hunched over the console watching the display on a little hand-held GPS unit that uses satellites to pinpoint its location. Pogy was sprawled in the bow, his dirty cap pulled down over his face. He stayed that way until we got to where the country widens out, the dense vine and trees of the swamp giving way to marsh grass and cattails along the banks. It's different up yonder, special with the feel of being so near that great inland sea called the Pamilico Sound.

Pogy responded to the change in the air by taking off his cap and running a hand as dark and gnarled as oyster rock through the sparse gray hair on his head. He pointed toward a clump of bullrushes growing on a small level point at a turn in the creek.

"There she is, cap'n."

Digger looked from the GPS to the bank, then told me, "Take the wheel." I did as he said, holding the bow pointed at the bullrushes while Digger reached under the console and pulled out a long camo scabbard. From the scabbard he gently withdrew a deluxe twenty-inch stainless steel Gerber machete, the kind they call a "Guatemala Toothpick," and tested it for sharpness.

"I thought we were going dolphin fishing," I said, knowing full well that any plans for the day were out of my hands.

"We are, soon as we're done here."

"Ever been on a pocosin?" Pogy asked in a ghoulish voice.

"A pocosin? Dammit Digger."

Pogy's crazy laughter cut me off. With a devilish grin in my direction he jumped over the bow rail and landed in an open spot on the bank.

"Wait!" Digger yelled, but it was too late. The only sign of our lunatic mate was a disturbance in the bushes, and then there was no sign of him at all.

"Crazy bastard. Good thing I've got the place marked." Digger held up his mobile GPS, then he jumped overboard too, "toothpick" in hand.

After a half hour's hike we came to an impenetrable tangle of green vines and twisted bush. At least it seemed impenetrable, until Digger began hacking a hole in it with the big Gerber knife. We bent low and slithered through, coming out onto a patch of ground solid enough not to be squishy under foot. So this is a pocosin, I thought.

73

The English explorer Lawson first wrote of "percoarsons" in 1709, and since that time the original Algonkian word has been roughly translated to mean "bog on a hill." That may seem a contradiction, but keep in mind that the crown of any hill in this country is still less than seven feet above sea level. Pocosins are rare and generally located miles from the nearest paved road, which is one of the reasons people use them for certain forms of agriculture—like growing the killer weed they call Pocosin Poison.

Sure enough, behind its tangled outer wall the pocosin on which we stood had been turned into a lush patch of hemp. The stalks were healthy, already forming iridescent buds that were waving in the breeze. Above the crop of boo stood a lone dead pine, its top snapped and its bark stripped off by some long-ago storm.

"Jesus, Digger!"

"It's somethin', ain't it?"

"Something like fifteen to twenty years."

"Aw, Dodge, you worry too much."

"Tell me you didn't plant this stuff."

"Hell, no. Pogy found it."

"So, what are you going to do about it?"

"I'm not sure."

"Whoever planted it is going to protect their investment." There had to be thousands of dollars worth of pot on that pocosin.

"I know. That's why I've been studying on what to do. Some way to collect on some of this found money."

"Digger, listen to me. Smoking this stuff is one thing, but you can't get into selling it. Forget you ever saw it, or you'll never get your captain's license back."

All he did was rub his head through the open top of his visor and stare at the crop of Pocosin Poison.

Pogy was waiting for us at the boat.

"Find any arrowheads?" Digger asked him.

He held one up for us to admire. A fine one, still sharp.

"Where'd they get the rocks," I wondered, "to make something like this?"

"Indians were traders," Pogy said. "Fish for tools, oysters for pots. That arrowhead prob'ly came from the mountains."

"Quit the history lesson and grab that line," Digger said. "It's time to get fishin'!" As we idled out of the creek he scrolled through the waypoints in his GPS. Satellites in geosynchronous orbit would guide our way to a spot with no road signs or landmarks. The Department of Defense went to great expense to build and launch those birds back in the '80s, and the system is, as they say, designed for multiple missions. Which is the government's way of saying that it's just as good for taking three yahoos to the Gulf Stream as it is for guiding a bomb down the mouth of some Afghan's cave.

Ain't America great?

I turned my cap backwards again and we came out into the Pamlico, then cut back through using a more traveled canal called the Thorofare. Back in Core Sound we turned due east and headed out Drum Inlet. Drum is a particularly shallow cut through the Banks, with very little water over its bar, but Digger knew how to read our way through that maze of breakers without running aground. Once we hit the ocean he headed south at about twenty knots. Behind us the Banks became a thin gray line and then sank below the horizon.

The brightest moment in running offshore is when you cross

into the hot blue water of the Gulf Stream, the longest, deepest, saltiest river on earth. We didn't need the electronics to tell us when we crossed the thermal edge. Across just a few yards of ocean the air warmed and I started coming out of my rain gear as fast as I could. The water beneath the boat was the definition of clarity, like looking into a diamond to see a spinning metal prop and bubbles rising behind it in playful twists. The Gulf Stream is precisely, deeply blue—a liquid sky, a pure reflection of the ocean of air above.

Pogy and I started rigging baits, frozen ballyhoo that had been thawed in a coating of rock salt to make them tough. With four baits skipping on the water we trolled back and forth near the temperature break. Digger glanced between his chart, temperature readout, and the Garmin GPS. For a few hours, at least, he could be Captain Davis once again.

When one of the reels started to squeal, I grabbed the rod while Pogy brought in the other lines in a well-rehearsed fire drill that clears the cockpit for action. It was a dolphin (the one they call mahi-mahi), a real road-runner that jumped three times, putting on a show in his skintight teal-and-yellow neon suit. When he'd been reeled to within an arm's length alongside the fish's overhanging brow gave it away as a bull of the species. With the fish seemingly under control, Pogy pulled on a pair of nubby yellow gloves stained red from previous encounters.

"Here's O.J.," Digger said, in a golf announcer's voice, "putting on his bloody gloves. Grab the leader, Juice." And he did, holding the twenty-pound dolphin in the water while I stuck him with the long-handled gaff and brought him over the side.

"Fish in the box," I shouted, a little too soon, because he'd slipped off the gaff before I could quite get him there. As soon as the fish hit the deck it went into a fit. A *gran mal* seizure, squared. A bull dolphin can swim at about fifty miles an hour for short bursts, and the fish loose in our cockpit used the same fast-twitching muscles to try to destroy the boat and everything in it. Somehow Pogy still held the leader; the O.J. gloves kept the line from cutting into his hands. Digger jumped into the fray using a lead-core billy club to whack the bull dolphin several times on its Neanderthal brow. Finally the thrashing stopped and the meat was in the cooler. The bloody cockpit looked like a piscine abattoir.

"That was some real purty work," Digger said, stowing his bloody club. "Let's get some baits back out there."

Once the lines were untangled and over the transom, I dipped a bucket overboard and rinsed the deck. Clear water eventually ran out the scuppers and I switched from swabbing back to fishing. We caught three more dolphin before noon without turning any of them loose on the deck. When there were no reels shrieking the soundtrack settled into the droning motor punctuated by radio chatter and the *snap-whoosh* of Pogy pulling the tabs on cans of beer.

At about two o'clock Digger decided that the bite was over. It was time to make a run toward home. Most of the day he had been busy at the wheel. Now, out in the cockpit, he glanced over his shoulder at the inshore sky and said, "Looks like we might get some weather." It didn't look like much to me, just the usual haze back over the beach. A different concern was coming off the conveyor belt in my head.

"We crossing the shoals on the way back?"

Digger nodded. We had trolled our way well south of Drum Inlet and the shortest route home would take us across Cape Lookout Shoals.

"Whatsa matter, Roger-Dodger?" Pogy teased me. "Scared of the shoals?"

"Hell no," I lied.

The Cape Lookout Shoals are a deadly finger sticking out more than ten miles into the ocean, a rolling alluvial fan of current-drifted sand where the bottom reaches for the sky and randomly re-directed ocean swells suddenly crest and smash themselves into explosions of white foam. The NOAA chart offers this official disclaimer: "Hydrography is not charted on Cape Lookout Shoals due to the changeable nature of the area. Navigation in this area is extremely hazardous to all types of craft."

That's good enough for me, but not for the local captains, who cross through a shortcut called "the slough." Buoys on either side mark the east and west entrances, but those buoys are false advertising for a route that isn't really a channel, only a slight depression in the shoals barely deep enough for a boat to zig-zag through.

I'd been there before, many times, but I still didn't like it when Digger set our course for the East Slough Buoy.

The morning's broken, high overcast had coalesced into a dark haze. As we started running a patch of that haze darkened into a thunderhead, resolving itself out of the wash like an image coming true on photographic paper. The wind was suddenly still and in the lull Digger applied more throttle to make time on the smooth sea. Then the wind started to pick up again, backing into the west. I kept my eye on that lone thunderhead, which seemed to be moving off inshore and to our north. I thought we had it made.

The first drops of rain were big, big enough to sting. And they didn't come from the cloud I had been watching, they came off an ominous dark wall that stretched from horizon to horizon in front of us. Back on shore, those with their cable TVs tuned to the Weather Channel had a better perspective than ours. They could see that what to me had looked like haze was the leading edge of a radar-returning red blob of strong thunderstorms stretching a hundred miles north and south, moving east at about thirty-five miles-per-hour. The storms spawned tornadoes and knocked down trees from Winston-Salem all the way to the coast.

We could see a curtain of rain coming, and when that hit us it was nearly black for a few heartbeats and then the world turned white. This storm had the same elements as any other—rain, wind, lightning, maybe a little hail. Yet in other storms I'd been in, I was more an observer of these events, and not so direct a participant. There is no harbor of refuge in the sea that's east of the East Slough Buoy, and there was no dry place on our center console boat. In a split second we were drenched. Sunglasses kept the saltwater from stinging my eyes, but I couldn't see through them and ripped them off. I hung onto the metal grab-rail so hard my knuckles ached. The wind sheared the tops off the waves, and even though it was raining sideways real hard, most of the water stinging me in the face was airborne ocean. On top of the wind waves the surface was a beaten white froth and the sky glowed eerily, the color of rotten meat. There was nothing for Digger to do but try to maintain a course into the wind.

Then the lightning closed in with thunder loud enough to make us let go of our handholds to cover our ears. Simultaneous flash-and-boom and no counting even one-thousand-one. Lightning so close you could hear it sizzling, so frequent you couldn't tell one bolt from the next. Holding tight to his helm, Captain Digger was all business. But Pogy, well, he was something else. He had no rain gear, of course, and he had pulled off his shirt and was standing bare-chested, holding on to the grab rail with one hand, clutching his necklace in the other. As the lightning bounced around us he threw his head back as if to drink the rain and began to howl like some wounded hound. Given our circumstances, it didn't seem like such a crazy thing to do.

Somehow Digger found the East Slough Buoy, which was good. But we also had to run the slough, through the storm-driven surf breaking on the shoals, and that struck me as a very bad idea. I asked Digger if maybe he wanted to circle the buoy and wait out the storm.

"Too much lightning!" he screamed above the wind. Then he steered a course to the west, into the wind. Into the shoals.

"*Hobbly-gobbly*," Pogy cried. "S'what the Ocracokers say." It was hobbly-gobbly in that slough, and then some. The two-ton boat jerked under us like a prodded rodeo bull while to either side of us waves crested face-to-face in spectacular explosions of spume. The water shot up in big chunks and we were close enough to experience the waves as solid blocks and to sense their negative space, too. To see and feel the holes that form in the water. The stern dropped into one of those holes; Digger pushed the throttle down until the prop caught and we climbed out slowly as if plowing through molasses.

Somewhere in the shoals we came out the other side of the storm. The lightning became nothing but thunder behind us, the wind dropped, the raindrops became discrete instead of a general torrent. We were still about twenty miles from the harbor, but we could see the lighthouse.

Digger's visor cap had slipped down around his neck, nooselike, his wraparound shades tangled in the strap. I slapped him on the back. "Thanks, man. You saved our lives."

"Weren't nothin' but a thang."

"I mean it." But instead of taking credit, he pointed to the homemade jewelry around Pogy's mahogany neck. The crazy old cowboy fingered his necklace and nodded, like he knew something we didn't.

"There's strong magic on these Banks," old Pogy said. "It ain't called the Graveyard of the Atlantic for nothin'."

Just then the VHF radio, good for nothing but amplified static during the lightning, returned to life.

"Mayday! Mayday!"

"Are you declaring an emergency?" came the voice of a Coast Guardsman at Fort Macon.

"Mayday!" was the only reply.

"Whoever he is, he's close," Digger said. While the Coast Guard radio operator kept trying without success to hail the "vessel in distress," Digger reached into his console and came out with a pair of binoculars. He handed them to Pogy and then got back on the wheel, carefully steering us around the worst of the hobbly-gobbly on the shoals.

"There they are," our lookout shouted. The white hull of the overturned skiff barely stuck out in the breaking surf, but the coolers and other contents were visible bobbing around nearby. Several orange lifejackets were mixed in the flotsam. Then Pogy noticed that one of them had a person clinging to it. On the radio we could hear the Coast Guardsman advising that a rescue vessel was en route, but obviously there wasn't going to be any radio response from the flipped skiff. The guy must have gotten his Mayday! off as he was going over. Without hesitation Digger turned away from safety and followed Pogy's pointing finger deeper into the shoals. When we reached the floating debris the guy in the water had managed to get his head through the neck hole in the vest. It took all three of us to drag him aboard, where he laid in the cockpit and immediately started calling for Evelyn. Getting up on all fours, he cried, "My wife!" and then began puking up seawater onto the deck.

Pogy went back into the pitching bow with his binoculars while Digger slowly circled the overturned hull, going out a little wider each time. We took several waves flush against the Parker's side, but with Digger at the wheel I never felt like we were in danger of capsizing ourselves.

The woman named Evelyn was floating face down, her long brown hair spread out in a slick of gasoline and two-cycle oil. She happened to be in a smooth spot between two bars where the groundswell was breaking furiously, and Digger angled the boat in alongside her.

"Grab the gaff," he said.

I got it out of the chocks and went forward with it, then leaned over and tried to snag her by the bathing suit that was tight to her body. But I missed. The bow bucked up and when it came down, I missed again.

"Jesus Christ, Dodge, hurry up." Just as she was about to be carried off into the whitewater Pogy grabbed the gaff out of my hands and in the same motion stuck her just above the elbow. The point of the gaff came through the fleshy part of her arm and he hung onto the handle while Digger put the outboard in reverse and slowly backed us out from between the jaws of death. I bent double over the gunwale and grabbed hold of the woman's leg. Together Pogy and I were able to lift her over the side, leaving a bright-red trail of blood from the wound in her arm. At the sight of his wife the husband passed out cold. I stuck the life jacket under his head as a cushion, then started to tie a rag around the woman's wound. That was fine until I saw her face, contorted and lifeless. I didn't even make it to the transom before I had to heave. Digger came back and put a hand on my shoulder.

"Take the wheel and let me deal with it. I've seen a lot more dead bodies than you have." Pogy got on the radio to the Coast Guard with the news of our partial rescue.

As we came out of the shoals a Marine helicopter out of Cherry Point, the one they call "Pedro," began to circle around us. A basket was lowered and we loaded the unconscious man to be winched aboard. The helicopter got out of there quickly, toward the hospital. We transferred the dead woman aboard the rescue vessel when it arrived. While a crewman on the Coast Guard vessel copied down Digger's hull numbers, the commander came to the rail.

"Thanks for the help, captain."

"Just following the rules," Digger said. "Rendering assistance to a vessel in distress."

"Hey," said the Coastie, "don't I know you from somewhere?"

"That was a long time ago." We shoved off from the high-sided rescue boat and headed back to Croaker Neck harbor.

chapter seven

A few days later I was nursing a cup of coffee in my kitchen when Shutterspeed came knocking at my screen door. Melinda was with him, and I invited them in for coffee.

"I heard you got caught in that storm last weekend."

"Yeah."

"Pogy said you had to pull a dead body out of the water."

"He did. I just helped."

"Stuck her with a gaff, he claims."

"I don't really want to talk about it."

"I can understand that," said Melinda, looking into her coffee cup.

"Not what I came to see you about, anyway." Speed held up a familiar green-and-yellow sheet of paper for me to see. "I'm curious about this 'Rally in Raleigh' business. And who's the Croaker Neck Seafood League?" The fliers I'd first seen in the harbor were spreading, from the fish house to phone poles, trees, and the front of nearly every house and trailer in town. I'd even seen a few duct-taped to the doors of some of the older pickup trucks.

Clutching the paper, the big man plunked down onto a wobbly chair at the kitchen table. The guy was huge but he had a piano player's hands, with fingers that were never still. Melinda's eyes were similarly busy. They searched about the small room, finally landing on Granddad's trunk over in the corner. He had bought the antique sea captain's chest from a dealer in Edenton. Even though I'd let the thing go, its age and value were obvious to Melinda. She ran her hands over the brass fittings.

"This has to be two hundred years old," she said with admiration.

"More. Its owner was a captain in Lord Nelson's navy, if you believe the woman who sold it. Go ahead and open it. It's still plenty sturdy."

Inside the chest was a jumble of Granddad's papers—stuff I hadn't looked at since his death, if I'd ever looked at it. Most of it was scientific language that didn't mean anything to me. An archivist from the university had contacted me about giving the papers to the library. I'd started to go through everything, intending to honor the request, but when I got to the old leather satchel full of his tools I lost the will to go farther. The university would have to wait, because no matter what was in that trunk, it belonged in Croaker Neck.

Melinda picked up one of the notebooks, flipped to the first page and read aloud Granddad's scrawled notation, *Raleigh's Colony at Cedar Island?* "What's this about?" she asked.

"A lot of the locals have this theory that the Lost Colony was really at Cedar Island, not Roanoke Island." When she gave me a blank look I said, "That's right at the end of the highway, here in Carteret County. The place where the ferry leaves for Ocracoke."

"Really?" She began to leaf through the pages. "Do you think I could read it?"

"Sure. But it's kind of a crackpot idea, don't you think?" She said something about historians getting things wrong all the time, and the crackpots turning out to be right. I offered to let her take the notebook with her.

"I wouldn't feel right about borrowing it," she said. "Everything in this chest must mean a lot to you."

"Then come on over and read it whenever you want. My door's never locked. But don't get your hopes up. That's like the ghost stories that float around in these parts. There's nothing to it."

"Looks like your grandfather took it seriously," she said, holding the book open to show pages filled with scribbled notes and diagrams. He had earned his reputation as an eccentric, after all.

Melinda took a seat on the floor, her back against the sea chest, and began reading.

"Back to this Rally in Raleigh," Shutterspeed said, insistently.

"The Seafood League represents the commercial fishermen," I explained. "And the real organizer of this rally is probably Ellis Vaughn, a lawyer who turned into the lobbyist for the seafood dealers. Everybody knows that the free beer and box lunches at these rallies are paid for by the wholesalers."

"Like the Fowlers over at the harbor?"

"No, the Fowlers struggle like everybody else. E.V. works for the big boys—the packers with fleets of trucks and connections all over. The Seafood League also sponsors fish fries and the Fourth of July parade. Not that you'd confuse them with the Kiwanis."

"Trouble-makers?"

"They might make trouble, all right, if you're one of those fish-hugging, sea turtle-loving, manatee tongue-kissing bastards that's trying to take away their way of life."

"You're kidding."

"I might be kidding, but they're not."

"Sounds interesting." He leaned forward and in a stage whisper added, "Pogy says there may be a secret mission involved."

I had no idea what Pogy could mean by a secret mission, but I did know that getting Shutterspeed mixed up with the Croaker Neck Seafood League would probably be a big mistake. Trying to head him off, I asked what this could possibly have to do with Virginia Dare. He claimed to be temporarily bored with the sixteenth century. "I need a little dose of the here-and-now. This gathering could turn out to be *Medium Cool* with white boots."

Since I'm not much of a moviegoer, Speed had to explain to me that *Medium Cool* is a famous film about the riots at the Democratic National Convention in 1968.

"Haskell Wexler wrote a script about a Chicago TV cameraman, then took his cast and crew to Chicago and filmed them 'acting' in the middle of the real riots. He shot scenes of his pretend cameraman shooting real cops busting real hippies on the head. They even got caught in real tear gas. The film came out in '69, right after I got back from the war."

"You were in Vietnam?"

"Taking pictures," he said, sipping his coffee. "I'd screwed up my shoulder in a car accident, so I had a deferment. But I was young and dumb and didn't want to miss the big show in Southeast Asia. Right out of high school I hooked up with a hippy magazine called *Cousin Jones*, which the Army in its wisdom thought was legit enough to earn me a press credential." Then I asked another simple question and he was off, telling me his entire life story. Or at least the part after he saw *Medium Cool*. He'd gone to film school at NYU, worked in public television, and scratched out a living making TV commercials. But he never got funding for the film he always wanted to make, the one about Virginia Dare.

"Why Virginia Dare?"

"I got hooked on the story when I was a boy, the day I saw Paul Green's outdoor drama, *The Lost Colony*."

I had been to Roanoke Island to see the play, too. Nearly every school kid in North Carolina at one time or another makes the trip in a yellow bus, which is probably why the play has had a run of about seventy summers. Shutterspeed didn't arrive at the Waterside Theater in Manteo on a school bus, though. He came from New Jersey with his parents, for a vacation at Nags Head.

"The Virginia Dare treatment stayed on the shelf while I accepted an offer to direct TV commercials for big and bigger bucks. I sold out for as long as I could, then one day I left Manhattan, drove straight to the Outer Banks. Moved into a motel and took long walks up and down the beach. I saw Paul Green's play every night for two weeks. From there I went to London, to the British Museum, to study the originals of John White's watercolors—the first images of the New World. Then I went to Seville and spent six weeks digging through the files in the *Casa de Contratacion* and the *Archivos de las Indias,* looking at charts and ships' logs, making notes. I went back to New York, sold my apartment, took all the money I'd made from commercials, and started the film.

"I'm getting close to her now," he said, staring blankly at my window. "Real close." Shutterspeed's eyes were shiny with the sheer emotion of his vision.

"That's a good story," I said, a little uncomfortable with his nearly religious fervor. "Now tell me why you're in Croaker Neck, instead of up at Roanoke Island."

"I started shooting in Manteo, but the place has been turned into a damned Elizabethan theme park overrun with morons in Beefeater costumes. Here I've got access to better locations in the National Seashore. Plus, studio space is less expensive."

"When you see this," Melinda said, indicating Granddad's notebook, "you might get some ideas about this place that go beyond cheap rent."

Shutterspeed ignored her and went back to prodding me about the Seafood League. "Are you going to get me into this Rally in Raleigh, or not? I'd like to document the event."

"What would you do with the film?"

"It will be video, not film. And you can tell your locals that I'll make them a copy. They can use it for PR, or home movies, or whatever turns their crank."

He crumpled the flier into a green-and-yellow ball and tossed it toward the trashcan sitting in the corner of the kitchen. His shot bounced off the rim and rolled across the worn linoleum floor until it came to rest next to his foot. He made no move to pick it up.

"Come on," he said. "We'll have fun. Right Melinda?"

Instead of answering, she carefully returned the notebook to the sea chest. After lowering the lid, Melinda stood up and brushed her hands together, a gesture that said, pretty clearly, "It's time to go." When Shutterspeed didn't respond, she started for the door anyway, saying she would come back to do some more reading as soon as she could.

"As long as I'm not imposing. . ."

"Any time." The screen door slapped shut behind her. I went back to trying to dissuade Shutterspeed.

"Look, you really don't want to mess with these guys."

"Aw, bullshit." He dismissed my caution with a wave.

"Don't let those official-looking posters fool you," I warned. "Ellis Vaughn tries to ride herd on them, but these boys in Croaker Neck are the type who like to sneak out to the government dock at night and put sugar in the game warden's gas tank. That fancy National Seashore headquarters is only there because somebody burnt down the government's original building."

"Somebody from Croaker Neck?"

I shrugged. The building had been destroyed right after the National Park Service started setting fire to the shanties on the Banks that the local families had been using as their fish camps for a hundred years. The officially-sanctioned arson was necessary to restore the habitat to its natural state. It was a tough lesson in the law of imminent domain that gave some of the hard crabs the notion that they could take the rangers to school, too. Or so the rumor goes.

"The radical fringe." Speed savored the words, and with a sinking feeling I realized that instead of talking him out of going to Raleigh, I'd made him fall in love with the idea. "So, who's this Bollard guy you mentioned?"

"Johnny Bollard. He's sort of a spokesman. Or agitator. Gus Ridge and the SCC pitch a fit whenever they hear his name. They think he's just another redneck with a chip on his shoulder. But Johnny's a good man. He believes he's doing right."

"Sounds like you know him."

"Sort of."

"Then call him," challenged Shutterspeed, getting up to leave at last. "Let him know I want to film his rally. Tell him I'll make him famous."

After picking up the crumpled flier from my kitchen floor, I decided I would let Johnny Bollard choose for himself whether he wanted to be in the movies. On the phone he asked me about the storm and said some kind words about Pogy, Digger, and me pulling the couple out of the shoals.

"Digger comes out looking pretty good in that whole deal, helping out the Coast Guard and all. If he would keep his nose clean, I believe he might be able to get his license back one of these days."

"*If* he keeps his nose clean," I said, thinking about the temptations of the plot of Pocosin Poison. "You know Digger."

"Yeah, I know Digger. I know he would rather fish that blue water than breathe. He'll get himself straightened out."

I told him the reason for my call, that Shutterspeed had an offer I thought he might consider. Based on what he knew about the dingbatter with the camera, his first answer was, "No way." But for some strange reason I tried to sell him on the idea. I'd been sold on it and now it had become some kind of screwy pyramid scheme.

"The TV stations are going to be there, and they're going to try to make you look like a bunch of redneck fools," I told him. "Maybe it wouldn't hurt to have some video that shows your side of the story."

"You promise me he won't cause any trouble?"

"What can he do? And besides, isn't that why you're going to Raleigh in the first place? To cause trouble?"

There was silence and I thought maybe the line had gone dead. Then Johnny told me, "I have to talk to E.V. first. Let me get back to you."

I knew that Johnny had more credence with the real fishermen than Ellis Vaughn, but he had to check with the money-man anyway. Two hours later I got a call back. "Bring the sumbitch," he said. "Just make sure you're there too, in case he does anything to piss me off."

chapter eight

The whole county was buzzing about what would happen in Raleigh. "Renegade Rally?" was the headline over an editorial in the newspaper. The writer questioned whether "a busload of rebels from Croaker Neck" was responsible enough to speak for commercial fishing interests. A front-page story quoted Ellis Vaughn saying that this was a friendly trip made at the invitation of the State Assembly, so how could anything possibly go wrong? A spokeswoman for the NC Department of Marine Fisheries said her agency would provide testimony before any legislative session at which their presence was requested. Representing the sport fishing interests, Gus Ridge of the Suburban Conservation Council managed to work his way onto the Greenville TV station, where he offered dire predictions that the Seafood League had a secret plan to disrupt traffic and bring the state capital to a halt. Some years ago, when this state still had tobacco farmers, a convoy of anarchist types in feed caps had done just that by driving their tractors around the freeway that circles Raleigh at five miles-per-hour. It was a bold move, but Ridge's suggestion that Croaker Neck fishermen could do such a thing was pure bull, and he knew it. An International Harvester tractor may be slow, but it's a whole lot easier to get to Raleigh than an eight-ton shrimp trawler.

While the media stew simmered, another turtle turned up marooned where it didn't belong—a rich lawyer's koi pond. The attorney, originally from Charlotte, bought an acre of land on the back side of Harkers Island and built, in the islanders' phrase, "the biggest house that's ever been." He hired a big-city landscaper to bring in plants and rocks and otherwise destroy any vestige of the natural vegetation that had thrived through countless storms and hot summers. Centered in the rock garden he built a koi pond, something like a swimming pool only for goldfish. So elaborate was the layout that it required the services of a full-time gardener, an older Asian gentleman who was probably the loneliest man in Carteret County. Upon finding a juvenile loggerhead floating Gulliver-like among his school of Lilliputian goldfish, the poor man had to be rushed to Carteret General with heart palpitations.

Ilse fumed; Special Agent Gatlin snapped his digital pictures while making his subtle threats in the direction of Croaker Neck. Finally I hoisted the bemused turtle aboard the *Gannet* for a ride back to sea. This time none of us missed noticing the hole in the edge of the loggerhead's shell. Not that we had any idea what to make of it.

In the midst of all the hype I went to see Shutterspeed to extend the invitation I'd helped to wrangle out of Johnny. Outside the old crab house scattered tufts of grass had begun to grow where the yard had been littered with junk, and Melinda had put out several pots of bright yellow mums near the doorway. The place had acquired a semblance of order, but the chaos was hidden in plain sight, too. For whatever reason, the Chevy van was no longer white—it had been re-painted in camouflage, the way duck hunters make up their old pickups and Jeeps. Maybe the movie director had legitimate plans for the duck season, but something about the new paint scheme struck me as all wrong.

Even more disturbing was Pogy's wooden skiff on a homemade trailer behind the van. The beat-up small outboard that had puttered him around for years had been replaced by a brand-new Merc with a jet drive where the propeller would have been. A jet drive pushes the boat with a powerful stream of water, like a fire hose. They're standard issue on the mullet boats that work the shallow flats behind the Banks. Pogy's new rig would take him across places where a bullfrog's ass would bump bottom.

Near the doorway the industrial-size generator roared. Walking inside the studio I saw Melinda on a brightly lit stage dressed up a little like Pocahontas against a backdrop of marsh grass and cattails. Inside that circle of light, she did not look like your chaste Disney Pocahontas, either. The way the buckskin costume hung loose on her long limbs had a certain slatternly appeal.

Behind the camera, Shutterspeed was all lathered up, yelling "Action!" and "Cut," and directing Pogy in the aiming of a dozen hot lights. Speed wore one of his loud Hawaiian shirts and an eye piece on a lanyard around his neck. Pogy was stripped to the waist and dripping sweat in puddles on the concrete floor. He was serious going about his work. With gloved hands he would adjust the angle of a light, then step back and judge the effect by tilting his head to the side and chewing on the fingertip of one leather glove. When he wasn't tilting the lights, he would aim a box fan at Pocahontas, who looked a little too warm in her bead-and-buckskin getup.

She was relieved to see me lurking near the doorway.

"Dodge, don't be shy. Come on in."

The faux Indian princess left her mark and walked over to greet me.

"Good timing," she whispered, "I was about to fry."

"Okay," Speed barked. "That's lunch!" The consummate professional, Pogy bellowed, "Let 'em cool!" as if he had a whole crew of lighting technicians under his command. He flipped a master switch and the stage lights went off all at once.

"What's with the costume?" I asked.

"I'm supposed to be Virginia Dare as a grown woman. Don't worry, you'll hear all about it." Then she told me, while we were still out of the others' hearing, that she needed to talk to me. When I asked her about what, she said, "Your grandfather's notebook. The Cedar Island theory."

By that time we'd gotten over to the set, where Speed immediately asked me, "What do you think of the grown-up Virginia Dare?"

"She's very attractive."

"*Aside* from the obvious."

"I guess I've always thought of Virginia Dare as a baby."

"Exactly!" He looked toward Melinda/Virginia, as if I'd just proved some point of his.

"We all think of Virginia Dare as a child. A child who's forever lost." Pointing his sandwich at my chest, he asked, "And do you know *why* has no one ever portrayed the grown-up Virginia?"

"Because . . . nobody knows what happened to her?" Nobody did, for a fact. Over one hundred colonists, and the baby, had vanished without a trace. But history-book history is never good enough for skeptics or true believers.

"Come on, Dodge, think!" I confessed that I had no idea what he was getting at. I also had no idea why he was getting so worked up.

"The reason," he said, leaning in now, very intent, "is that Virginia has to remain a *virgin*! Otherwise the story of her birth won't work as America's nativity scene. America's myth-makers don't want you to picture Virginia Dare making it with Indian studs." Behind him, Melinda rolled her eyes. Shutterspeed was beginning to sound like one of the grassy knoll, black helicopter crowd you hear on late-night radio.

"Captain Pogy has been showing Will some amazing things back in the marsh," Melinda said, trying to cut the rant short. I wondered if those amazing things might have included the pocosin filled with pot. If so, Digger would not be pleased.

"I noticed Pogy's boat has been upgraded a little," I said. "You wouldn't have financed that fancy new motor would you?"

"There was some money in my shooting budget for transportation," Speed said, sounding almost defensive about it.

"Well, you won't have to worry about running aground in that rig."

"That's the idea. We were just about to wrap here and go for a little ride. Care to come along?"

"Sure he's coming," said Pogy with a wink. "Ain't you Roger?"

We launched the revamped boat at the ramp in the harbor. Luckily it was quiet, but the few regulars who were at the docks didn't hesitate to point and laugh at the Chevy van's new paint job. Pogy shot them a one-finger salute and over-revved his new motor. Before we embarked Shutterspeed hung a camera around his neck, one with a zoom lens only half as long as a bazooka. Without bothering to explain he handed me a pair of Zeiss binoculars, and we were on our way.

Pogy gunned the Merc and the jet outdrive bubbled furiously behind us as we shot across the sound and headed straight toward the Banks. We ran between some PVC stakes—the gold standard in homemade channel markers—and up a shallow creek on the back of the Banks. In a brand-new fiberglass boat the effect would have been exhilarating. Cowboying around like that with Pogy was more of a thrill ride than I'd been looking for. After flushing some gulls off their marsh island rookery, we turned a couple of figure-eights and then roared out of there again, headed back the way we'd come.

"How do you like her?" Shutterspeed yelled.

"Fast," was all I could say.

"I got me a real shit 'n git rig now," Pogy agreed as we approached Murdock's Island.

Thanks to the marshy ground and large number of snakes Oscar Cruz's survey had been going slowly. Only a few acres of the forest had been cleared, with the slash piled and ready for burning at the east point—which seemed to be where Pogy was headed. Where the marked channel turned to the right he swung left and hugged the contour of the land as we circled halfway around. When the throttle suddenly shut down I thought we might have run out of gas, but as soon as we had coasted to a stop Shutterspeed stepped over the side and waded out onto a patch of beach a few yards square. Without a word he snuck off into the underbrush with the camera around his neck, skirting the surveyors who were working so near to us that I could hear their voices. Pogy used the burbling jet-drive motor to move us a short distance away.

When I asked what was going on, he put both hands up to his eyes, imitating binoculars. "Watch for his signal."

Scanning with the Zeiss binocs didn't reveal much except glimpses of the surveying crew in their blaze orange vests. Two duck blinds were near either tip of the island. A tottering structure closer to the center looked like it might have once been used as Murdock's hunting camp.

"Have you and Digger been back to that pocosin?" I asked.

"Nah."

"How about you and your movie-making buddy?"

"Nah." When I asked him what the big guy was doing out there now, with his camera, he said, "Takin' pictures."

A white ponytail came bouncing through the bay myrtles and Shutterspeed stumbled down the tiny beach and into the water. I started to alert Pogy but he'd seen him already, gunning the motor so quickly that I fell over backward into the boat. We jetted directly up to where Speed was frantically waving and took him aboard, then started heading west along the shore. At the island's western tip a V-hull boat with blinking blue lights on its T-top came heading our way. Pogy reversed course and hugged the island so tight that we ducked for cover under low-hanging tree limbs. The bigger, faster Marine Patrol boat had to keep its distance, running out off the edge of the flat and parallel to our course. The sight of a tall Black guy hanging onto the T-top raised the hairs on the back of my neck. When we came off the east edge our jet boat snuck between two marsh islands before the bigger craft could run us down. It finally occurred to me to ask why the hell we were running from the law.

"I was trespassing," Shutterspeed said. I didn't think anyone would call out the Marine Patrol for trespassing on a construction site, but something had gotten them in high gear. When we shot out through an opening in the marsh the chase boat was again on our flank, this time with nothing but open water between us and the Banks.

"When's low tide?" Pogy asked.

I looked at my tide watch, the one I'd given Granddad on his final birthday.

"It's two hours past!"

"That's at the inlet," the old cowboy said. "Back in here, it's still falling. With this little bit of nor'east wind . . . there should be just enough."

Enough what?

With the patrol boat about to catch up, we arced along the edge of a shoal so shallow that a group of gulls was standing on it. We seemed to be headed for the channel that led to an abandoned duck club. One of the largest buildings still left in the National Seashore, it could sleep nearly a dozen hunters in each of its two wings.

Pogy jerked the tiller left and then right, and the skeg under the jet drive just barely bumped one edge of a protruding bar. Swinging us around until we had a clear view of the pursuing patrol boat, he cut the throttle back to idle. Pinned between the shoal and the Banks, with just the one channel, he'd turned us into sitting ducks. As Shutterspeed calmly filmed the lawman's boat bearing down on us, Pogy told a story.

"My daddy was the caretaker of this fancy club for a while. When the sports were off in Charlotte or wherever it was that they lived, we'd come over and hunt from their blinds, which used to stand right about here. Once Daddy and I had shot our limit of redheads, and then some, and out across the sound I could see a boat headed straight for us. Daddy was gathering up the decoys and I warned him about the boat, asked him who that was, coming on us so fast. And he says, 'That's the new game warden.' So I'm thinkin', shouldn't we be high-tailin' it out of there, us with them illegal ducks? But he just keeps pickin' up the decoys and pretty soon he looks out toward that boat and says, 'Watch this.'"

Just as Pogy got to that part of his story the Marine Patrol's big outboard motor made a choking sound as the prop hit bottom in that oh-so-false channel. The hull abruptly settled off its plane, hard aground. I looked through the binoculars long enough to confirm that it was Special Agent Gatlin who'd gone tumbling towards the bow along with two state Marine Fisheries cops. Thankfully no one looked hurt, but they would be stuck there at least three hours, until the tide switched and floated them off.

As the cops scrambled to regain their footing, Pogy picked up his story right where he'd left off. "'That's the *new* game warden,' is what my Daddy said. He knew that spot on the edge had shoaled up—in Hurricane Donna, I think he said—but the warden didn't." Finished with his tale, he threaded a course through the maze of marsh islands, keeping us close to the grass and out of sight.

"I don't know why you ran from them," I said. "And I probably don't want to know. But there's a federal agent on board that boat who's going to try and tear all of us a new one. And you two ought to know that." Not surprisingly, neither my captain nor his camera-toting mate seemed chastened.

"It's maneuvers," Shutterspeed explained. "Before the main mission."

chapter nine

The main mission began with a dirty tin charter bus idling in front of the post office, where several local fishermen were shuffling around on the broken pavement, looking down at the oil stains and drinking coffee from Styrofoam cups. Different patterns of camo shirts were on display, everything from Mossy Oak to Realtree. A few of the Seafood Leaguers wore their work clothes: the standard white boots topped by rubberized bibs stained with fish slime. A person more cynical than I am might say they had dressed to impress the legislators in Raleigh with their authentic Old Salt costumes. On the other hand, the closets in Croaker Neck aren't exactly overflowing with suits and sports coats.

A coffee urn was set up on a card table next to the receiver-less payphone, and tending it was Peggy Fowler, from the fish house.

I took a steaming cup out of her hand. "Where's the ringleader of this circus?"

"He's here somewhere," she said.

"You going to Raleigh with us?"

She made a noise through her nose. "I got no more business in Raleigh than you do," she said.

"Mornin' Roger-Dodger." I turned around and saw Pogy reaching for a cup of coffee, too. He had dressed in long pants for the occasion—the kind that turn into shorts when you zip the legs off. His T-shirt warned me to "Shut Up and Fish."

Johnny's black Ford pickup was parked behind the bus. Hitched to the truck was a red-and-white wooden skiff with its deck piled high in net. The boat was identical to the one Johnny and I had grown up fishing from—it had to be the one Big John had spent the last year of his life building. I started to walk back there, then stopped long enough to help Digger wrestle a heavy cooler through the door of the bus. The Igloo was covered in "Number 3" Dale Earnhardt stickers.

"Have you been back up yonder?" I asked him.

"Where?"

"To the pocosin," I whispered.

"Nope." When I asked him what he planned to do, he just shrugged and said he'd make up his mind when the time and the crop were ripe.

At the back of the bus Johnny was jury-rigging a trailer hitch onto the bumper using C-clamps and a length of logging chain. He got up brushing his hands against the sides of his jeans. The Cat hat on his head looked brand new.

"Where's your Hollywood buddy?"

"Not sure. What's with the bumper hitch?" To answer Johnny pointed behind us, where Pogy and three other guys were taking the trailered skiff off from behind the Ford and wheeling it up to be secured on the back of the bus. They reminded me of the Roman legionnaires wrestling with their catapults in *Ben Hur*. The trailer they dragged was homemade. Saltwater cowboys are famously handy with welding gear, and in a Saturday afternoon they can slap together a boat trailer out of some re-bar, four lengths of pipe, a set of hubs, and two mismatched tires—which often as not come from underneath somebody's new mobile home. They seldom bother with taillights or a license plate. Usually they'll spray on some primer to slow down the rust, so the classic Croaker Neck trailer is reddish-orange, like a bad hot dog. There's one in almost every yard.

I asked Johnny why he was taking a skiff full of net to Raleigh.

"Can't catch votes without a net, son. Gonna park it right at the state capitol! That oughta get their attention." He reached into his boat and pulled a bumper sticker from a cardboard box. "Jesus was a fisherman," it read. "And *He* Caught Fish With A Gill Net." A small logo was down in one corner. A variation on that cartoon fish the Christians favor, only this one was wrapped in a net. Pogy used his sleeve to clean the soot off a patch of the bus bumper, then pasted the pseudo-psalm over the rusted chrome.

Will Shutterspeed walked up just as the last boxes of fried chicken and biscuits were being loaded. He had one arm around the video camera on his shoulder, the other around Melinda's slim waist. The boys stopped inspecting their box lunches long enough to get an eyeful of Melinda. She looked sporty, in tight black jeans and a black T-shirt. Her hair was tucked up under a cap with *Panavision* stitched across the front. On closer inspection, the arm around her waist didn't strike me as affection; more like her mentor was corralling her. Maybe she wasn't so keen on going along after all. Melinda looked so squirrelly that when Speed stuck his hand out toward Johnny, I thought she might bolt. Instead she turned her attention toward the man in the Cat hat just as Shutterspeed was saying, "You must be Johnny." The movie director had cranked up a smile with the kind of wattage successful people use to get rich, elected, or laid. The man always seemed too big for whatever room he was in, was loud and liked to show off, but when he wanted to he had a way of looking at you that could disarm a charging bear. Charisma, maybe, or just a gift for bullshit. Whatever you want to call it, I saw it work on Johnny Bollard as at first he hesitated, then shook hands.

"I've seen you around," Johnny said. The Cat hat came off and he shook hands again when Shutterspeed introduced Melinda.

"Johnny," Speed said, "I thought maybe you could ride with us in my van, let me get some background material so I know where to focus when we get to Raleigh."

"Is this on the record?" Johnny looked at Speed dead seriously, then punched me on the shoulder and broke into a smile.

"I heard a guy on *60 Minutes* say that. 'Is this on the record?'" Shutterspeed laughed, and Melinda smiled. Two could play this charisma game, it seemed.

"Dodge says you want to film our side of the story."

"That's right."

"I don't suppose you ever commercial fished."

"I haven't fished at all since I was nine years old. And that was at Camp Sunnybrook."

"Camp Sunnybunny, huh?" Johnny said, and sort of winked at Melinda. "We got one of them camps right down the road here, maybe you heard of it. Call it Camp Lejuene." I expected Shutterspeed to say something about his Vietnam experience, but he let it ride.

"I guess it wouldn't hurt to ride with you," Johnny said. He walked over to the front door of the bus and told the driver to go on. The bus took off in a cloud of diesel dust, towing the skiff on its orange trailer. In the big Chevy van Melinda and Johnny sat in back. On the passenger side Shutterspeed turned the swiveling captain's chair around so he could point the camera toward the rear, at Johnny's head. I drove, and listened to the interview going on behind me.

"Where do I start?" Johnny asked. Later, hearing him on the videotape, I realized the years of smoking Kools had given his naturally smooth voice a bluesy tinge. He sounded a bit like a honky Lou Rawls.

"You're involved in shrimping, right?"

"I trawl for shrimp, that's right. I've run a hundred crab pots at one time, haul seined for trout and croaker, kicked clams, and done tree work for the electric co-op. Been chief of the volunteer fire company, too."

"How did you lose the tip of that finger?"

"I was bluefinnin'."

"Tuna?"

"That's right. The big ones that come in the wintertime. The buyers pay ten bucks a pound at the dock in Beaufort and ship them to Tokyo."

"How big are the fish?"

"The one I lost my finger on dressed out at a little over three hundred pounds."

"And how did it happen? Your finger?"

"Oh, we were hauling the fish on board in a big sea and I slipped up. A swell went by, the deck dropped out from under me, and the line looped around my finger. The fish jerked and the end just popped off."

Melinda said "ouch" and made a face.

Johnny's voice shrugged. "It happens. Lots better'n being pulled overboard. That happens, too."

"Tell us about your family."

"My family was Bankers. They lived over at the cape, settled there even before there was a place called Diamond City. They caught whales, and melted their blubber down for lamp oil in big cauldrons right there on the beach. The whalers here didn't leave home in sailing ships to hunt whales. They posted lookouts on the high dunes and watched for the whales to swim by. When the lookouts saw one, the whalers would launch their boats right off the sand and row after them. Usually six men on the oars, a harpoon man in the bow.

"You're not supposed to talk about it now, but they killed more porpoises and bottlenose dolphins than whales. Thousands of 'em. Could you imagine what would happen now if they saw you peelin' the hide off old Flipper and chunkin' his blubber into a big pot?

"When my buddy Don was in the Coast Guard I went to New Bedford in Massachusetts one time to see him. That whole town was like one big museum for whaling. But when I tried to tell those Yankees that my family had been whalers, too, down here on the Banks, they looked at me like I was crazy."

That was the end of the interview, but it's not the end of what Johnny had to say that day. As it turned out, he was just getting warmed up for the show he put on in the chamber of the State Assembly.

The Croaker Neck Seafood League's lawyer, Ellis Vaughn, had called in any number of favors to set up Johnny's speech to the legislature. I'm not sure if old E.V. knew what he was doing or just got lucky. Maybe a little of both. The legislators, along with the media in Raleigh, may have been expecting an uneducated redneck, but Big John's kid from Croaker Neck gave a speech that held the attention of every person in that exquisitely paneled room. Those city people listened to Johnny's bluesy, gentle voice like he was telling an exotic story from some far-off land.

When he was introduced by the Speaker, Johnny walked to the front and stood a little awkwardly between the North Carolina flag and the United States flag. The dark-suited men and pink-suited ladies of the Assembly applauded politely. Remembering where he was, Johnny quickly took off his Cat hat, tilted his head down, and smoothed his graying hair. He stared at the floor for an uncomfortably long heartbeat or two, like maybe he was going to freeze up. But then he ran his hand through his hair again, laid the hat down next to the microphone, tilted his face up, and looked at everyone in the room with blue-green eyes that sparkled like the sea. Maybe in his mind Johnny did see the water and not the room full of puffy faces staring up at him.

"Let me start by saying that everyone in our group is his own man, and I wouldn't want you to think that I speak for everybody. One of the reasons we fish in the first place is that we can't stand to have a boss."

He smiled, and a few of the poobahs chuckled.

"There's a war going on, against the way we live and how we make our living. Maybe it started back in the sixties, when the state of North Carolina began buying up the private land on the Banks. Folks who had deeds to the prettiest beachfront property in the world got paid a dollar an acre! Then, in the seventies, Cape Lookout National Seashore gobbled up the Core Banks and Shackleford, those sand islands where my ancestors were both born and buried. They tore down our fish camps. They closed the two Coast Guard stations, which once provided a lot of jobs. And they've got all these rules about where and how a man can fish, where he can shoot, even where he can let his dogs run.

"In the end the National Seashore has been a good thing because it saved us from being turned into Myrtle Beach. The reason I bring it up, though, is that it was Downeasters that were asked to sacrifice for the good of everybody. We didn't have a say in the matter."

I looked around the balcony, where visitors sit in two rows of church pews and look steeply down into the well of the Assembly chamber. The troops in their boots and rubber bibs took up two rows. In the next section was a class of school kids on a field trip with two teachers watching them like buzzards on a wire. A Highway Patrolman stood guard at the door, holding his Smokey-the-Bear hat under one arm.

"We do plan to have a say in what happens next, though. In my short lifetime I've seen the end of tobacco farming and textile making in this state, and I'm determined not to see the end of the seafood industry. Not while I'm still alive. But many people seem intent on making it so a man can't make a decent living catchin' fish or shrimp. And they're doing it by using the sea turtles and the Endangered Species Act.

"It would take me all afternoon to tell you about all of the turtles I've seen, if I could remember them. I've seen loggerheads big as Volkswagens. I've seen Kemp's Ridleys, green turtles, all the rest—because they live where I work, in the ocean and the sounds. Somehow they've always made their way, even when it was still legal to shoot them or knock 'em on the head to make soup.

"Then the environmentalists got into the act. People with second homes, a lot of them brand new to our state, formed these groups and started hunting up every turtle nest on the beach, roping them off so nobody would disturb the eggs. Come the new moon in October, when the eggs hatch, the beaches are full of tourists making sure the baby turtles get down to the water safe and sound. As if the turtles haven't been finding the water on their own for a million years or so. Of course, the people who organize these turtle hatches don't ever tell the tourists about how the sharks and red drum are waiting there in the surf, ready to have a feast with the little buggers."

One of the school kids let out an "ewww," and was shushed by her teacher.

"That's just Nature taking its course," Johnny said, as if to that little girl.

"Now, I'm not here to tell you there's anything wrong with getting all weak in the knees over baby turtles. They *are* cute. But I will point out that these are the same people who have paved over the beach for their condos and motels. I *will* mention that when it rains the runoff from all that pavement carries oil and chemicals into the salt marsh, where it destroys the habitat for fish and shellfish. I *won't* say what happens when all of those people in those condos on the beach flush—you can figure that out for yourselves."

Another "ewww." Another *"shush!"*

"We all have been trying our level best to live with the turtles and the turtle people. By law every shrimper has turtle excluders, which are basically big holes we cut in the trawl net to release the turtles we catch by accident. The government's made regulations, and we do our best to follow them. At the same time, the government turns a blind eye to how many turtles were killed to catch the tons of shrimp that get imported into this country every day. Almost ninety percent of the shrimp eaten in the U. S. of A. is imported, and nobody cares how or where it was caught."

Digger may have thought he was whispering when he said, "Damn right," but I saw the Highway Patrolman flinch, and heard one of the teachers instinctively utter a "*shush.*"

"The problem is," Johnny continued, "some people won't be satisfied until every turtle in the ocean dies of old age, and that is never going to happen. It's not Nature's way that it would.

"But the shrimp trawling issue is more or less settled. For now. The reason we're in Raleigh right now is that the turtle lovers and the Suburban Conservation Council want to force the federal government to stop us from gill netting flounder in the Pamlico Sound. They say there's too many . . . 'turtle interactions,' is what they call them. Maybe they haven't stopped to consider that the only reason we're interacting with so many turtles is that there's more of them now than ever before. Or, maybe they considered that but they don't care. Maybe their real aim is to stop us from netting any way they can."

"That's right!" It was Pogy this time, nearly shouting. Johnny glanced up, but didn't break stride.

"There are entire agencies devoted to saving the turtles, and more agencies that want to replace fishing with aquaculture. Are we going to let them?"

"No!" the chorus answered from the front row of the balcony. Looking back over my shoulder, I saw the trooper put his free hand on his nightstick.

"And what about these so-called conservation groups, that want to turn the sounds and the ocean, that belong to everyone, into playgrounds for the surfers and recreational fishermen?"

"Stop 'em!" cried the gallery.

"What kind of person is it who puts one man's sport over another man's livelihood? Save the turtles?" Johnny hollered. "We already saved the damn turtles, now who's going to save us? Who's really endangered here? Us, or the turtles?"

Down below the Assembly members began to get skittish. Striped ties were adjusted and skirts began to rustle. On the words "damn turtles" the kids in the gallery giggled.

"Unless we get some respect in our own state, unless someone helps us get the government off our backs, we're the end of the line. Y'all will be eating farm raised shrimp from Louisiana or flown in from Brazil, and the North Carolina fishing industry, the *American* fishing industry, will be a thing of the past."

The two rows of Croaker Neck fishermen stood as one, yelling and waving their caps above their heads. Taking their cue, the schoolkids started to join in, but the two teachers quickly hustled them out the door, giving us teacherly scowls.

As the kids filed out I saw Shutterspeed head for the front of the balcony, where he knelt down and started rolling tape. On the way in he'd been warned by the cop that videotaping in the chambers was not permitted, but the trooper had exited ahead of the sixth graders, possibly going for reinforcements. Below us, the legislators craned their necks around to see who was causing the commotion. You've never seen so many bad comb-overs in your life. Johnny stood squinting up toward us, too, still standing in front of the chamber, holding his hat in his hand. Then the Speaker went up and banged his gavel for quiet, quickly shook Johnny's hand, and showed him to a side door. I was already headed toward the exit myself when the rest of the boys got the idea. Good timing, because the trooper came through the balcony door with two more big guys in gray wool uniforms behind him. They were wearing, not holding, their Smokey hats, like maybe they wanted both hands free. I thought they might grab their batons and start wailing away, but the fishermen were all acting like good soldiers now, and they marched single-file past the itching cops. Even Digger kept his mouth shut. Down by the front pew of the gallery I saw the little red light on Speed's camera wink out.

Waiting on the sidewalk were camera crews and blow-dried reporters from the Raleigh, Greenville, and Little Washington TV stations. Johnny walked right past them to his skiff, which had been rolled into the plaza in front of the Legislative Building. Johnny put a foot up on the trailer tire and vaulted inside the wooden boat. The rig was parked right on top of a mosaic of the North Carolina state seal, a blue circle set large into the concrete. As the TV crews assembled below Johnny, they stood on the state motto. *Esse quam videri*—To be, rather than to seem.

From his perch knee-deep in the spongy white gill net, Johnny gave a soundbite version of his us-or-the-turtles speech, looking the part that I knew he felt deep in his bones. A small crowd of civilians was gathering. Johnny Bollard became a fisher of men.

"We're the last of our breed," he said, "We are descended from the men who cast their nets with our Lord on the Sea of Galilee."

I looked around, and every face was turned up toward the barrel-chested man with the Cat hat tilted back on his head. A few of the city dwellers were wearing sideways smiles, but nobody was laughing and few were able to walk by without stopping at least long enough to politely take a bumper sticker. Melinda was giving them out with tremendous enthusiasm and a look on her face that reminded me of those Hare Krishnas you see in airports. She'd been converted all right. And from appearances so had Shutterspeed, who was crouched way down so he could shoot the Seafood Savior with nothing but the Carolina blue sky for a backdrop.

Johnny quoted Genesis—Pogy's bit about the 365 bones in a whale's mouth—and just when I thought he'd gone completely Primitive Baptist, that he might reach down into the net at his feet and come up with a rattlesnake to handle, he came to his senses and quit. He thanked the crowd and climbed down out of the boat wiping sweat from his forehead. All the boys pounded him on the back and pumped his hand. Melinda dropped bumper stickers on the sidewalk and gave him a big hug and Speed got that on videotape, too.

When the TV news crews had rolled up their cords the rally was officially over. Melinda, Shutterspeed, and I went back to the van. Through the windshield I noticed Johnny off a short distance on the lawn, talking to a round, white-suited man in the shade of a big oak tree. I recognized E.V. by his bow tie and Colonel Sanders suit. The lawyer-lobbyist handed over an envelope, shook hands, and started walking away. Johnny glanced inside the envelope, then quickly stuffed it into the back pocket of his jeans. Grinning wide, he walked over and stuck his head inside the bus, then hustled over to where we were sitting. I looked around to see if I was the only one who had seen the envelope exchange. Speed was fiddling with the camera; Melinda was lying across the back seat, resting her eyes. She sat up with a start as Johnny climbed in, breathing like he'd just run the four-minute mile.

"Follow the bus," he said, pointing. "We're headed to the best steakhouse in town." He reached around and pulled the envelope free. Fifty-dollar bills were spilling out of it, and I noticed several hundreds keeping them company.

"Hope y'all are hungry!" he crowed.

We drove to a place on the edge of Raleigh called the Steer Barn. Famous throughout the state, the Steer Barn is more than a restaurant: it is a compound of faux farm buildings set in a small pasture, a theme park devoted to the display and consumption of beef in all its forms. When our mixed-up little parade—bus, boat, van—pulled up in the courtyard, the brown cows grazing inside their barbwire pen didn't seem to notice, but the three white-jacketed parking attendants sure did. Two of them approached the door of the bus, then jumped aside to avoid getting trampled under a horde of white boots. The third attendant stood up—he'd been on one knee, polishing the barbwire with Brasso—and ran off inside. Maybe to dial 9-1-1, I thought. But E.V. must have called ahead to grease the rails. Even though the *maitre de* looked to be in shock, he managed to lead us through the quiet restaurant to a private dining room at the far end. Except for the staff setting tables the house was empty. It was barely six o'clock, an ungodly early hour to be entering the Steer Barn. Unless, of course, you were a commercial fisherman on shore leave, with a lifelong habit of getting up before 5 A.M. and having supper on the table by 5:30 in the evening.

Truth be told, most Croaker Neck fishermen are a church-going lot; but not all, and not always. As soon as they saw that our private room included a bar, complete with bartender, a few of them walked over to put their white boots up on the brass rail. In the middle of them, jawing away, stood Will Shutterspeed, taller than Digger and as big around as Johnny Bollard; he was the only one in the room sporting a white ponytail. I watched as

Speed knocked back a shot of brown liquor, then leaned over and said something to Digger, who threw his head back and roared with laughter. The bartender poured a double shot of expensive Scotch for Pogy.

Johnny elbowed his way through the bunch at the bar to set a cold bottle of Bud down in front of me. I started to make a place for him at the table but he was already on his way over to a different spot by the window, where Melinda sat alone. Very smooth, I thought. Talk to the new recruit while her boyfriend is busy being one of the guys.

Then the food started coming, in mass quantities. Everyone enjoyed the long, rowdy, beefy meal—even if the staff seemed to forget the way to our room halfway through. Maybe we got off to a bad start with them when most of the crew ordered their New York strips and prime rib well done. "Burnt," is how Dan Fowler wanted his. When the food was delivered, just about every cowboy at the table started shouting, either for ketchup, A-1 Sauce, or Bac-o bits for their baked potatoes.

Finally the effects of pounds of beef and gobs of sour cream began to outweigh the booze and adrenaline. The noise died down, and one of the waiters got up the courage to bring in the dessert cart. Three hours after we'd taken the private room and its bar by storm, our busload of boat jockeys strolled back out through the restaurant as quiet and polite as a group of insurance salesmen, expense-account fed and sucking on their after-dinner mints. But even if they'd been dressed up in Armani suits I'd have known them by their walk. Every one of them weaved between the tables on the rolling gait of a man with lifelong sea legs.

I watched Johnny settle up with the head waiter. Even after he'd paid our tab and flipped the bartender a fifty-dollar tip, there was so much cash left that he had trouble stuffing it all in his pocket. How much had E.V. given him?

"Where's Melinda?" I asked him instead.

"Girl's room, I guess."

"You know, she's sort of spoken for."

"Mind your own business," my friend suggested. But then, like people often do, he encouraged me to do just the opposite. Sidling up next to where I was leaning my back against the wall, he asked me, "Where does your Hollywood buddy get all his money, for fancy cameras and crab house renovation?"

"He made it on TV commercials."

"Is that what he told you?"

"Yeah. You hear different?"

"It's Melinda's got the money, bud. She's got the looks *and* the money. He was in hock up to his ass."

"What'd he do, impress her with some Hollywood connection?"

"Don't think so," Johnny said, looking at his well-chewed toothpick. "I think she's in love with the crazy bastard."

"How'd you find all this out?"

"I asked her," he said. Then, deciding to rub it in, he added, "Just ask, my friend. That's all you got to do."

Maybe that's true, if it's your day to be the Seafood Savior. The rest of us mortals are forced to learn these things second hand.

chapter ten

When we got outside the boys were walking around in the dusk, having an evening smoke. Except for Pogy, who wasn't walking so much as he was being carried by Digger and Dan Fowler. The old maritime monk had carried on drinking the fancy Scotch a little too long. His handlers kept a firm grip, heading their staggering cargo toward the Chevy van instead of the bus.

There was something about seeing Digger in Raleigh that made my unease over the Pocosin Poison farm grip me by the back of the neck. Back home it was easier to view the whole thing as a lark—a little harmless fun growing back in the marsh. Being in the city reminded me that there are cops and judges who take such things a lot more seriously.

I promised myself I'd find a way to keep him out of that ditch.

As Dan and Digger loaded their drunk into the far-back bench seat, I saw Johnny and Shutterspeed walking across the parking lot to the back of the bus. Had Johnny crossed the line by cornering Melinda during dinner? Was Shutterspeed drunk or crazy enough to start something in the middle of the seafood soldiers?

But there was no fight. Johnny simply leaned with his forearms resting on the gunwale of his skiff; the ponytailed moviemaker stood with one foot up on the trailer tire. Just two good ol' boys who might have been talking about the Talladega race or the weather. Johnny's hands idly dithered around in the mesh of the gill net, and Speed nodded his head a couple of times. Then they walked to the back bumper of the bus, bent as one, and lifted the tongue of the trailer off the makeshift hitch. Those who had been milling around the bus pitched in and they began wheeling the trailer and skiff in my direction. The load landed on the van's hitch ball with a thud that bounced the Chevy on its springs. Digger, Speed, and Johnny got in without saying a word to Melinda or to me. Pogy was quietly mumbling in the way-back.

Something was up, and I seemed to be the only one in the dark about it. Standing outside the van's open sliding door I had the same sinking sensation that I get climbing aboard a boat on a morning when the weather service has already put out small craft warnings. On those days you keep telling yourself you don't have a choice, and after a while you believe it.

"Get in, Dodge!" Speed said from the driver's seat. "We're burning daylight."

"It's already dark. In case you haven't noticed."

"That's just an expression," he said impatiently. "Get in."

"Why are we towing the skiff?" I asked.

"We're on a mission," Shutterspeed said.

"How's that?"

"Just get your ass in here," Johnny said. Long conversations always had bored him.

"Come on, Dodge," Melinda coaxed me. "It'll be fun." She already knew. Obviously Johnny had filled her in at their cozy corner table. He'd told her about "the mission," she'd bartered back the inside scoop on Virginia Dare financing.

The charter bus lurched out of the lot and made a right turn, toward home. I wished I was on it. "Your other ride's already left," Digger said. "Better get in."

I took the seat next to Melinda on the middle bench and slammed the door home on its track.

"Roger-Dodger," Pogy mumbled in the seat behind us. "On a mish'n."

Like many other modern Southern cities, Raleigh is Atlanta Lite, circled by "the beltline," a six-lane Interstate racetrack with downtown on the inside and the suburbs on the outside. Most of the inside is about what you'd expect: decaying neighborhoods, public housing, old warehouses, shuttered supermarkets and broken-glass parks. But one slice of that inside-the-Beltline pie doesn't empty out after dark. That slice is Old Raleigh, where the real money in the Capitol City lives. In Old Raleigh the quiet streets still run under the crowns of the 200-year-old trees that gave the town its Chamber of Commerce nickname, The City of Oaks.

We were driving down one of those winding streets, past houses so grand that the expression "a ton of bricks" might describe a single wall. Soft porch lights spilled over lawns as smooth as pool table felt.

"Are we lost?" I asked. That's what any sane person would have thought, seeing our van pass in the night, followed by its ghost ship full of net.

"I got my bearings," Johnny growled. "At this stop sign turn right, then pull into the first parking lot you see." The sign at the parking lot entrance read *City of Oaks Country Club*, and the lot was predictably full of Mercedes, BMWs, Saabs, tricked-out Jeeps, and Japanese SUVs. I noticed that most of them had red decals in the back window. A pattern that looked familiar—concentric red circles with a star in the center. They were all members of the SCC! Sure enough, a banner hanging over the entrance to the low brick clubhouse welcomed one and all to the Suburban Conservation Council's annual fund-raising banquet.

"This isn't going to bring the Law on us, is it, Johnny?" Instead of answering he stepped on my foot on his way out the sliding door.

"Dodge, you're in it. Unless you want to go inside, with the rest of the hook-and-line fishermen." Johnny pulled Pogy out of the back seat, reached in again, and dropped a bundle of Jesus-used-a-net bumper stickers in my lap.

"I'd like to see one on every car. Wouldn't you?" Then he held out more stickers for Melinda. "You want to pick up Dodge's slack, if he chickens out?" She numbly took the bundle from Johnny's hand, but her and her eyes were focused on the white ponytail hanging over the back of the driver's seat.

"Will?" Melinda said. "This won't jeopardize our project, will it?" She sounded genuinely curious, ready to go either way. Shutterspeed turned around, and there was a half-smile on his face—so studied that he must have been using the rear view mirror to get it right.

"*Medium Cool*," Speed said, as if those two words explained everything.

Watching her face in the weak glow of the dome light, I saw taut muscle under the soft outline of her jaw. Maybe it was the way she turned her head, or maybe the light shifted a little, because her eyes had become brimming pools of liquid. Johnny had been right. She *was* nuts about the guy.

Shutterspeed glanced at me, trying to involve me in his fantasy, too. In his mind it had become *his* mission now. Melinda turned her glow in Johnny's direction, and asked him, "What are you guys doing while Dodge and I stick bumpers?"

"Cap'n Hollywood here's gonna learn how to set a net. Now you two get busy." The way he was looking at me, his face full of mirth, there was no way I wasn't going, just like he said. I started laughing as I got out of the van.

"Damn it, Johnny, you've been getting me in trouble since I was ten."

"Weren't for me, you would never have had any fun in this life." He clamped a hand down on my shoulder. "And don't you forget it."

Melinda took her bundle of bumper stickers and disappeared into the rows of cars. I went the opposite direction, crouching down, peeling and slapping as I went. Briefly, I wondered which make of luxury SUV would have the most sensitive alarm system. On one Volvo wagon I pasted over a sticker that read *Save the Loggerheads.* From inside the brick building came a cloud of hearty guy laughter. Maybe the banquet MC had told a joke. Possibly the one about the game warden and the redneck fishing with dynamite. Along with the cloud of laughter came the smell of the sportsmen's cigar smoke, which overpowered the honeysuckle growing wild on the perimeter fence.

After I'd finished about a dozen cars I stood up to stretch. Sighting across the top of a red BMW Z3, I saw the white Chevy pass down a lane between cars, and behind it Pogy, Digger, and Johnny were standing in the stern of the skiff, paying out net over the transom. In the harsh mercury-vapor parking lot lights, they seemed to be throwing a train of spun silver overboard, where it billowed in their wake.

They had started by fastening one end of the net around the bumper of a Land Rover. By keeping the net taut they were able to catch at least some part of every vehicle they passed—aerials, hood ornaments, door handles, license plates. Shutterspeed kept driving at a steady four knots or so, and the pros in the boat were laying it out as naturally as if they were floating a spring tide in Cape Lookout Bight. I heard Pogy say something about having "the right marsh to catch a Subaru" and the others all laughed.

When the last of the net flew out the stern Johnny whistled and the van stopped. Realizing they had me wrapped up with the vehicles, I panicked and ran for it. At the edge of the lot I tried to hurdle the net, but when my foot caught in the float line, I fell and skinned my knee.

"You all right, buddy?" It was Digger kneeling down beside me. He helped me untangle myself and I limped beside him up to the skiff, where the rest of them were standing on the empty deck laughing at their handiwork. I climbed in, too, and looked out to see a parking lot full of four-wheeled boys' toys caught in the gill net just like a school of jumping mullet. It was going to take the SCC hours to cut themselves loose.

"I hope they brought their fancy Gerber pocket knives," Johnny hooted.

A splashing noise came from the stern of the boat. Pogy was pumping his bilge, and a stream that only a racehorse or a drunk fisherman could produce was wetting the canvas top on some hard-luck sportsman's Miata convertible. Melinda started giggling and Pogy looked over his shoulder in shame.

"Sorry ma'am," he said, continuing to hose down the Mazda. "I forgot you was with us."

"Carry on, cap'n," was all she said.

Once we'd climbed down Johnny unhitched the trailer in such a hurry that the tongue kicked out a few sparks when it hit the pavement. He insisted that we leave his skiff and trailer right where it was, blocking the parking lot entrance.

"But that's your boat," I protested. "Big John's boat."

"It gives me bad memories," he said. "Besides, if we try to tow it home the Highway Patrol will catch us before we get off the Beltline."

"What if they trace it to you?" Shutterspeed asked.

"It's hand built. No numbers."

"Yeah, but it's one of a kind, too." Digger was actually doing some thinking.

"Plus," Shutterspeed said, "It's covered with fingerprints."

"I never been fingerprinted," shrugged Johnny.

"Well, I have," objected Speed. Digger said that he had, too.

"Argggggghh," Johnny said, and reached under the skiff's bench seat, pulling out a red plastic gas can. A few seconds was all it took to splash enough liquid inside the skiff. We all piled in the van, the driver's door wide open and the engine running. A minute later Johnny was running, too, and the wooden boat went up with a *whoosh* behind us. It was burning bright when we rounded the corner, the glow inspiring even the reckless Shutterspeed to drive at a law-abiding speed.

At the Johnston County line Digger pulled out a pint bottle of bourbon and started passing it around. I volunteered to drive so that Shutterspeed could indulge along with the others. Johnny had one swig but then said he needed to keep an eye on me. Shutterspeed, with a good buzz going, said we were "a real bunch of monkey-wrenchers." I was relieved when all of the passengers except Johnny finally passed out.

It was long after midnight when we hit the stretch of shoulderless two-lane that runs through the marshy land between the North River and home. After a hundred and fifty miles I was still checking the rearview mirror between heartbeats.

"They're not coming after us," Johnny said quietly. I looked in the mirror again, at a different angle, and saw that Melinda's Panavision cap had slipped off into her lap, and her slender neck was crooked with her head leaning on Pogy's shoulder—a sight he'd later ask me to describe to him so many times and in such detail that eventually he believed that he'd seen it himself, and been awake to feel her pressed against his side.

The moon illuminated a thousand bright ribbons of water threading through the dark marsh grass. They shone as if every oyster in them was a Christmas tree bulb. Johnny tuned the AM radio until the soothing sound of Skip Carey's voice filled the cab with Braves' baseball, a late game from out on the other coast. I glanced into the mirror again, to make sure the passengers were still asleep. I desperately wanted to confide in Johnny, to tell him about the pocosin and ask him to help me talk Digger out of whatever he might be planning.

"You think he'll get away with it?" Johnny asked.

The back of my neck felt suddenly cold. Was he reading my mind, or did he already know that Digger was thinking about ripping off the Pocosin Poison?

"Who? Get away with what?"

"Whoever it is that's been messing with these turtles." My grip on the wheel relaxed a little.

"You don't know anything about it, right?" I asked him.

"I told you that before."

"Good thing. There's this federal guy—"

"Marshall Dillon, huh?"

"Something like that. I think he's got plans to lock somebody up. If that somebody was from Croaker Neck, it wouldn't break his heart." We rode along in silence for a few miles. Finally I asked him if he'd ever broken the law.

"The SCC's going to claim I just did."

"I mean a serious crime."

"Arson's serious."

"Burning your boat wasn't arson. More like a funeral pyre. Wasn't that how the Norse seamen were supposed to go out—set adrift in a burning boat?"

"Christ, Dodge. Big John was no Swede."

"It's not like you're going to file an insurance claim," I said bringing the conversation back to crime.

"Wouldn't," he said, smelling his fingers for traces of gasoline. "Even if I did have the insurance."

The Braves game changed to static. He reached over and clicked the crackling radio off, in the same motion laying three hundred-dollar bills on my right thigh.

"What's that for?"

"For writing my speech so good."

I glanced in the mirror: still full of sleepyheads. The work I'd done for Johnny was supposed to be our secret.

"I didn't write any speech. Just looked over what you already had."

"You did more than that. And it worked so good, E.V. said to put you on the payroll."

"The payroll?"

"He's got a notion I might run for county commissioner. In which case I might need more fancy speeches."

When I laughed at that, Johnny pushed his Cat hat way back on his head, turned and looked at me. The moon shone on his high-and-getting-higher forehead, and his face had its own network of little creeks running across it. The watery blue light in his eyes had long since ebbed, and I wondered how much longer he'd be living his tough life on the water.

"Why's that funny?" he asked me. "I'm a pillar of the community. Got a wife and two kids, don't owe too much money."

"You're right," I said. "Why not? After all, this crime spree you've been on is sure to give you one hell of a head start in politics."

"Well, roger that," Johnny chuckled.

Knowing that E.V.'s offer was the local equivalent of the kind you can't refuse, I stuffed the three bills in my pocket.

"Nobody can find out I'm working for the Seafood League, you know."

"Afraid you'll lose your turtle gig?"

Life is full of surprises, and the biggest are those you pull on yourself. For some reason, instead of ratting out Digger I confessed something completely different.

"Living without Ilse is driving me nuts."

"You think that's a secret? Plus, old buddy, it's not been real great for the rest of us. Since the two of you stopped screwing each other, she's been trying to screw every fisherman in the state."

"So to speak."

"Whatever."

"You know, Ilse has always had nice things to say about you."

"Look, Dodge, I know she's a sweet woman, and awful good-lookin', but I've never seen a grown man as love struck as you. And here she's thinking about going in with Gus Ridge and the SCC to near-about ruin Croaker Neck. Damn if it don't strike me like she's the enemy."

"You don't know the half of it," I said.

"Meaning?"

"You remember the day I met her, when she came in the fish house and I took her to the cape?"

"Sure I remember. I won ten bucks off Dan Fowler. What happened out there, anyway? A rich woman shows up, she's just passing through, and the next thing we know you've got her moved in on Ballast Creek."

"It's kind of a long story."

"We've got a few more miles to go."

"Well, that day a southwester blew up and the ocean was rough as a cob. But she had to get to the cape anyway. So I tied up at the old Coast Guard dock and we walked across. With a bottle of wine. Everything was going great until she asked me about the gun mounts. What was I supposed to say?"

"It might not have been a bad time to make something up," Johnny suggested. "You're pretty good at that."

chapter eleven

But I didn't make anything up. What I said was, "The Germans *were* the enemy, and in these waters they were doing most of the killing. With torpedoes."

"Yes, torpedoes." She was squinting into the sun, and I couldn't read her face. Then she used her hand to shade her eyes, turned and looked at me.

"Did you know that by the summer of 1942 the U-boats had sunk more than two hundred ships in American waters?" She recited this statistic like it was something she'd learned well, and a long time ago. "This was done by only five German U-boats." She took another swig of wine, killing the bottle.

"Are you proud of it?" I challenged.

"Proud?" She asked the question of herself, then answered it, "Yes. I am." Sounding as if it surprised her.

I let that lay for a few minutes, until I said, "You know, I heard the U-boat stories, too. Only from the other side." Our side.

In the winter after Pearl Harbor the U-boats started attacking within sight of East Coast beaches and by March of

1942 the night sky along the Banks was frequently lit by burning cargo ships. The German wolf pack had its biggest successes hunting the North Carolina capes, where the freighters and tankers could be pinned against the shoals. They were sitting ducks.

I was eleven years old when Big John first took me to the gun mounts. He told how the artillery pieces had been set up there in the fall of '42, too late to save the tanker *Naceo,* torpedoed less than a mile off Shackleford Banks. Gasoline from her hold burned on the water for days. I still remember the catch in his voice when he told us how twenty-four sailors had died within sight of the beach. The same beach where I now sat with the German woman named Ilse.

She took the empty wine bottle and began letting sand trickle into the neck from the palm of her hand. She concentrated, and then, as if speaking to the sand, she said:

"My uncle served on the U-124, under *Korvettenkapitan* Johann Mohr. The greatest ship killer of them all, if my uncle is to be believed." She paused a moment, and played in the sand. "But Uncle Friedrich was not an easy one to believe.

"He was a great teller of tales. When I was young I believed all of them. Then I got older, and I discovered things about him. That he had girlfriends, sleeping around on my aunt, the woman who had raised me. So I began to hate him. Him and his stories. 'How can you be a war hero,' I wanted to know, 'when your side loses?' Yet everyone seemed to believe the big U-boat hero. All except me. I suppose knowing this bothered him a great deal, because when he died, he made sure that his most prized possessions went to me."

Somewhere in the telling of her story Ilse had started to cry. She reached into her leather bag and her hand came out holding a tissue with something wrapped inside. She carefully unfolded the tissue and placed in my palm a small circle of gold with a war eagle at the top, a swastika where the bird's feet would have been, and below that a detailed miniature submarine, complete with a tiny cannon mounted ahead of the conning tower.

"Uncle Friedrich's submarine war badge," she said. Then she used the tissue to wipe the tears off her cheeks.

"When I was a girl, and he was very old, my uncle told me of seeing the lights of American automobiles through the periscope. He even told me about the wild ponies. But my uncle's most fantastic story, the one he told only late at night after many schnapps, was about how he had invaded America. One night when the moon was new Captain Mohr surfaced the boat near a place called Cape Lookout.

"Mohr was supposed to be the bravest and the craziest of all the U-boat captains. It was said he had *Fingerspitzengefuhl*— the touch. According to my uncle's story, on that moonless night in March, 1942, Captain Mohr ordered one of the lifeboats inflated, and he sent the men ashore, four at a time, to invade America, and then row back to the U-boat."

"That's nuts," I said. "Wouldn't it be in the history books?"

She stopped fidgeting with the wine bottle, which was now full of sand.

"I didn't believe it, either." She reached into her bag and pulled out a much smaller leather pouch. The tanned surface was cracked from age, but it was easy to make out the swastika that had been tooled into the leather. I watched as she dumped the contents of the pouch into her hand, filling her palm with a mix of white sand and coarser dark bits. She put the leather pouch aside and scooped up beach sand with her other hand. Holding the two together in front of her face, she went on.

"Of all the crazy stories, *this* was the one I could never believe.

'You have never invaded America!' I told him. Then he would get out his pouch, and show me the sand. 'The sands of Cape Lookout,' he would say."

She looked up at me, her eyes shining, her face an ocean of calm. She held her upturned palms together in front of me. The sand from her uncle's pouch looked just like the beach we sat on.

"I was wrong, don't you see?"

I watched the ocean, wondering at all of the hardship and heroism and just plain waste that had been swallowed up in it. The ocean swallowed them all indiscriminately, as far as I could see, and left us only our memories to sort out one from the other.

Ilse let the sand funnel back into the pouch from the bottom of her hand. By now the edges of the sun were sharp as it hung just above the horizon. It would be dark before we got back to the boat.

Johnny had been silent as my story ate up miles of road, but when I paused, not really wanting to get into the personal part, he took it upon himself to cut to the chase. "So," he said, loud enough I was afraid he might wake the others in the back of the van. "You rigged it so the two of you had to spend the night on the boat."

"Not the boat. The old lifesaving station."

"Ah. Smart move. Not exactly the Holiday Inn, though."

"We made the best of it."

"Oh, I'm sure you did."

"Remember, I had a twenty-dollar puppy drum on ice back in the *Gannet*. And a pint of brandy, in case of emergency."

"Which this was obviously turning into . . . ."

131

No one had used the place in years, and with the southwest gale blowing up above, the fireplace in the nineteenth-century, Cape Cod-style lifesaving station didn't draw very well. When the driftwood fire I'd cobbled together burned down to a bed of glowing coals, I showed Ilse how to grill the fish using its thick scales as a natural roasting pan. We ate dinner with our hands and took sips of brandy between bites.

"This is delicious," Ilse said, licking her fingers. She looked oddly at home sitting in front of the hearth on a life jacket. I sat off at the edge of the firelight in an old government chair, the cane bottom rotten and ready to give way under me. The wood I'd rounded up wouldn't keep the fire going much longer. We'd start to get cold—maybe cold enough to huddle together for warmth.

As if reading my mind, Ilse threw two pieces of driftwood on the fire. As she did an odd but pleasant thought sparked in my brain.

"Ilse, did you really miss the road to the ferry by accident?"

"Of course. What do you think, that I went to Croaker's Neck on purpose?"

"It's Croaker Neck. And isn't it a little bit strange that you and I could be here by accident?"

"We were in your boat. You made the decisions."

"That's funny. I don't feel like I've had much choice in any of this."

"An accident, or not," she countered, "we are here. Must everything happen for a reason?"

As she said this she was fidgeting with the silver ring on her finger. The ruby glowed like an ember that had burst out of the fire and landed on her hand. She noticed I was staring at the ring.

"The money is my husband's. I suppose I could get half. But I might get nothing at all."

"You want to tell me about it?"

"I've already said enough. Right now I don't really give a mouse's ass."

"Rat's ass. You don't give a rat's ass."

"Right," she said, and laughed a little. "He has a rat's ass."

I started laughing too, and she turned and looked at me. She'd pushed her hair back on one side, and it glowed in the firelight. "*Red*," Peggy had called her. But the haughtiness that had attracted me and irritated Peggy, that was all gone. Ilse's chin was no longer arguing a point with gravity and the years she had seen were now plain for me to see, too. Her beauty was soothing by its very waning. She'd come so far and yet had the perfect face for that season in that place.

I got up off my broken chair and went over to sit down on the floor beside her, using the tarp as a cushion. She leaned into me and laid her head softly on my left shoulder.

"Your grandfather is dead now?"

"Yeah."

"How?"

"He fell off his own dock and drowned."

"How odd," she said, taking my hand in hers. "My uncle survived an entire war in a metal tube under the water . . . ."

"And Granddad drowns in the creek." The fire needed more wood, but I didn't want to move, ever again, if Ilse would keep holding my hand like that. She looked at me. Not sleepy, just dreamy.

"Tell me, what are you doing working at the end of the road, shoveling ice on pregnant fishes?"

"I go there to pick up girls. It would surprise you, the number of beautiful women I've met there."

"How many?"

"At least one."

"Stop teasing me." She looked at our two hands. "I told you my uncle's secret. Now it's your turn."

"Here's a secret: This island that we're on, all of these great Banks of sand, are constantly moving."

"It's just the wind."

"Oh, this whole cape is moving, all right." Ilse let go of my hand.

"So the place where my uncle stood when he invaded America, it's gone now?"

"Not gone. Just moved to a different spot. When I was a boy those gun mounts were high up on the beach, but now at high tide you can barely see them. Won't be long before the ocean swallows them completely."

"Nothing stays the same," she said to the fire.

This time I took her hand and squeezed. "We could," I hoped out loud. "We could stay the same."

By that time our van-load of monkey-wrenchers was passing the outskirts of Croaker Neck. Everyone in back had slept through my story, and Johnny had been so quiet that I thought he might have been dozing, too. But he'd been following it, all right.

"So," he said, "You gave each other aid and comfort."

"What do you mean?"

"That's what they call it, you know: Giving aid and comfort to the enemy."

chapter twelve

Ilse did turn out to be the enemy, but not because her uncle invaded America, or, the way Johnny saw it, because she valued turtles more than people. She became the enemy of my heart. She made it a P.O.W. and then brazenly ignored the Geneva Conventions.

We stayed together for the best part of one blissful year, or just about two months longer than it took for her lawyer to get the divorce finalized. At that point she became very independent, both financially and otherwise. She bought a vintage house on Ann Street in Beaufort, just down the street from the Old Burying Ground. She moved out of my cabin gradually, the way a tide ebbs, and my keel settled to the bottom so softly that I hardly noticed being stuck in the mud until it was too late. For another month or two we still dated, which at first meant Friday and Saturday nights in the historic district for me. Then it started to mean a few arguments inside and outside of Beaufort bars. By that time Ilse was moving up in the civic ranks, serving on the Historical Association, the

Friends of the Maritime Museum, and then becoming president of Tortugas Now!.

"These scenes of yours are no good," she said, referring to an argument we'd had the night before, outside the Velvet Elvis saloon.

I apologized, of course. By that time I was apologizing every day, for something.

Then one night I tried to touch her, and in a voice that sounded rehearsed she told me, "That part of my life is over." Something she couldn't explain to me. So she said. Almost overnight, the energy she'd once had for me—for sex—was transferred to the crusade she'd chosen for the second half of her life: saving the turtles.

Logically, I could convince myself that our affair was nothing more than the final rejoinder in a long-running argument she'd been having with herself over leaving the rat's ass of a husband. And I should have known from the beginning that a woman like Ilse could never settle down in Croaker Neck.

But what's the role of logic when an exotic redhead has your heart locked up in solitary?

In spite of myself, I had to admire the way she fit into the culture of Beaufort, which was growing more cosmopolitan every day. And Ilse was a force in everything going on. She never let the fact that she was new in town, with a German accent, slow her down. With no real ties, Ilse was free to make the friends and enemies she wanted, and every time I saw her was a painful reminder that she still had all the charm, the beauty, and honesty that had attracted me in the first place. When she offered me the job carrying turtles back to sea, I jumped at it.

But to Johnny, Ilse was becoming a real enemy, and I was determined to do something about that. Despite what he sometimes said about her, I always believed that deep down he respected her. And that she returned it. The Seafood League should have known that Gus Ridge and the Suburban Conservation Council's lawyers and lobbyists were the real threat, along with men like Oscar Cruz who would drive up the price of land and property taxes, too. But the turtle huggers made more convenient targets.

In my own eyes, writing Johnny's speech for him hadn't put me on one side or the other. He'd asked me to help and I didn't see any way I could say no. But taking money from Ellis Vaughn was another story altogether. As much as I could have used the money, I put those three hundred-dollar bills in a drawer, determined to let them be until this whole affair was settled. I had every naïve confidence in the world that it would be settled, too. I just had no idea how.

When I started looking around for someone I could trust, a party with no axe to grind, the person I found was Melinda. She was sitting on the cabin floor, next to Granddad's sea chest, reading in his notebook about the Lost Colony. The book, among all the contents of the sea chest, had piqued her anthropologist's curiosity.

I poured us two glasses of iced tea and told her there was something I needed to talk to her about.

"If it's about you writing Johnny's speech, I know all about it."

"How—?"

"He and I had a long talk at that restaurant, remember. Right before we went out and netted a parking lot full of cars." Okay, so maybe Johnny couldn't keep a secret, not when there was a pretty woman on the listening end. But I still wanted her advice.

"See, I've got this problem," I began, but she cut me off again.

"What do you know about this theory that Cedar Island was the real Lost Colony?"

"I first heard that crazy story when I was still a kid."

"Well it might be more than just a tall tale."

"Maybe Bigfoot is, too."

"Be serious for a minute." Leafing through the notebook, reading some of Granddad's notes out loud, she boiled down what he'd written so that even I might understand. As usual, the Professor had been thorough in his research. He cited the written record left behind by John White, the colony's governor and Virginia Dare's grandfather. Going further, he'd looked into the original English land grants in what became Carteret County.

According to the notebook, Granddad was inclined to believe the theory that Sir Walter Raleigh's colony was not established on Roanoke Island, but on Cedar Island, which is about seventy-five miles south of there. He thought that the "River Occam" described in Arthur Barlowe's 1584 journal may have actually been Core Sound. Narrow and long and flowing into the much larger Pamlico Sound, it could have looked just like a river to the Englishmen.

Toward the end of the notebook Granddad went on a tirade over the way any evidence that might have backed up the Cedar Island theory had been destroyed by the State Department of Transportation. For centuries the Indians shucked oysters, scallops, and clams and tossed the shells into piles that grew to astounding sizes. The piles remained largely undisturbed even after the Indians were long gone. But when automobile travel finally came Down East, the state used its trucks and heavy equipment to distribute the piles as a crude paving material.

"Those shell middens would have been full of artifacts," Melinda said with no little hint of disgust. "People were driving cars over the record of an entire culture!"

"Well, there's not a lot of gravel down this way."

Ignoring that lame excuse, she read me the last paragraph of the notebook, which was a series of three questions. "Was the Lost Colony ever really lost? Looking in the wrong place all along? Are their kin still living Down East?"

"Wow."

"Wow is right. It gives me goose bumps just to think about it. That your friends Johnny, and Digger, and even Pogy might be descendents of Virginia Dare."

"Now there's a thought to bend your mind. But, speaking of those guys, I wanted to ask you for advice, remember?"

The fact that I'd written Johnny's speech didn't seem to trouble her.

"You were just helping out a friend."

"But Ilse's my friend, too."

"More than a friend, I'd say."

"Come on, Melinda. Help me out."

Finally she put down her reading and looked up at me. Her time in Croaker Neck had given her sailcloth skin only the faintest hint of a tan.

"You shouldn't feel guilty about being on both sides," she said. "Maybe where you really are is on the common ground. Instead thinking of it as 'playing both sides,' why don't you try to bring them together?"

"Maybe because I don't want to get caught in the middle."

"You're already 'caught in the middle' simply because of the facts that you know. Facts nobody else has."

"You have them. You know more than I do. For instance, I'll

bet you know what Shutterspeed was filming on Murdock's Island, and why NOAA and the Marine Patrol chased us halfway to Ocracoke that afternoon."

But she refused to talk about that, no matter how I coaxed. She would protect Shutterspeed at all costs—a fact I needed to file away for future reference.

The man in the middle—how could I make that work for me? I was sitting on my dock, wondering about that, when the gentle south breeze brought me the irritating noise of a poorly muffled small engine. It wasn't the pleasing hum of an outboard, but the rattling of a portable generator on Murdock's Island. The generator powered a garish red Coke machine that had been ferried over to the otherwise deserted island and plugged in right next to the brand-new dock and shade shelter.

Beyond the Coke machine and makeshift landing, I could see Oscar's surveyors busy bush-hogging lines through the brush so they could finish siting the condos and marina that would turn Murdock's Island into A Sportsman's Paradise. Smoke rose from smoldering piles of slash too green to properly burn. Work was still going slowly because of the snakes—a detail that Oscar would surely keep from the eager-beaver realtors who would soon be riding across the channel to "walk the dirt" and get cold drinks from his Coke machine.

The vending machine was worse than just a nuisance—it had become a hazard to navigation. One night Digger, on his way home by boat from the Dock House bar in Beaufort, mistook the blazing Coke emblem for a red channel marker and nearly ran smack into the island. That incident might have raised some local hackles against Oscar; but people said it *was* Digger after all, and went right back to respecting private property. Even as the project took shape directly across from the harbor, Croaker Neck was still biting its collective tongue. But I wondered how my neighbors would react when Oscar started running his realtor ferry service, and the harbor-side parking lot became clogged with the minivans and Mercedes SUVs with out-of-state plates.

Over in Beaufort, the Tortugas Now! membership seemed not to care one way or the other. I had mentioned the travesty to Ilse, and, knowing well the view from Ballast Creek, she'd been properly outraged. But anyone who could read a chart knew the glaring Coke machine wasn't visible from the Beaufort waterfront on Taylor's Creek. They would never have a view of Oscar's condos, which were not, after all, in *their* back yard.

From my dock, I saw the *Lady Ann* go gliding into the harbor. As I watched Johnny pilot her into his slip, I got an idea. Not a plan, exactly, but just a glimmer of hope that I could do some good, here in the middle.

The glimmer of hope started to coalesce into a plan later that night, when Ilse called about a Kemp's Ridley turtle in the back of the Beaufort mayor's pickup truck. The smallish turtle was found floating inside a 192-quart Igloo cooler, with three cans of Bud keeping him company.

"Dodge?" she said, before hanging up. "There's a hole in the back of its shell."

The Igloo turtle was the easiest rescue I ever made. At the town docks, the flustered mayor simply backed his truck right up to the *Gannet's* side. The only thing tough about it was the crowd of gawkers, made up of the tourists and yacht trash who flock to Beaufort's waterfront on the weekends. Agent Gatlin must have been off for the day, but two town cops and two National Wildlife Service agents handled crowd control. They didn't notice the quarter-sized hole in the turtle's shell, and Ilse didn't say anything to them about it.

"Dodge, this has got to stop!" she said when the cops and crowd had gone.

"Don't you think I'd stop it if I knew how? Or knew who?"

"You're certainly getting your share of attention."

"Are you accusing *me*?"

"No, no. I'm sorry." She genuinely was, and in her moment of weakness I saw an opportunity to invite her to come on board.

"Just until you leave the dock."

"Agreed. I just need a chance to talk to you, is all."

"Talk about what?" she asked, taking her familiar seat in the cabin, on top of the engine box. My memories got the better of my doubts and out came the opening lines of my half-baked plan: "Johnny Bollard wants to take you for a ride on his shrimp boat."

"Why would he want to do that?" She was immediately suspicious. I never was a very good liar, so I started talking fast, rushing my words as I explained to her how, if she was going to go to court and claim she knew something about shrimpers and turtles, she at least ought to see how a trawler works. See the turtle excluder devices in action.

"And this was Johnny's idea?" she asked, still skeptical.

"Absolutely," I lied.

"What about the speech he gave in Raleigh? I saw him on TV, preaching about how Jesus fished with a net." That clip was some of Shutterspeed's finest work. Working the phones together with Ellis Vaughn, we'd gotten it picked up by CNN, ABC, and PBS.

"That was just politics."

"I should have known Johnny would make a good politician," Ilse admitted. "The speech must have been good, because eight different state legislators left me phone messages. They want to hold a hearing."

"You know Johnny." I shrugged.

"The SCC called, too." Her gray-blue eyes were locked onto my face like radar.

"Johnny says you ought to stay away from Gus Ridge," I said, finally delivering his message.

"Maybe you should leave him alone, as well. I understand someone disrupted their big fundraiser." She *knew* I was in on the net prank. She couldn't, but she did. I started rummaging around at the helm, making noises about how I needed to get the turtle back in the water.

"Please be careful, Dodge." This time she sounded like she was thinking about my well being, not just the turtle's.

"I will," I promised, "if you tell me that you'll think about Johnny's offer. It wouldn't hurt you to learn something, you know."

"If he talks to me directly, I'll think about it," she said, turning to climb onto the dock.

It didn't take me long to realize that in order to make my plan work, I would need Shutterspeed's help. If I could have done it without him, I would have. But his camera was the ingredient that would make this gumbo thicken. Getting him on board the *Lady Ann* to shoot video for more good PR was my best hope for selling Johnny on the idea I'd already sold to Ilse as *his*.

Over at the crab house there was no sign of Melinda and Pogy was busy with the movie gear, giving me an opening to bring up my plan to Shutterspeed in private.

"I've got a notion we should get Ilse Brunner out on Johnny Bollard's shrimp boat," I dangled, hoping the "we" wasn't too obvious as bait.

"Why?"

"To make peace before one of these turtles gets killed and a real war breaks out." When he still hesitated, I stretched the truth a little more, telling him it was really Melinda's idea.

"So, this is a set-up for one of our underground news releases." The guy loved anything with even a hint of the secret and sinister.

"Well, I don't know if it's exactly 'underground,' but yeah, that's what I had in mind."

"A great idea!" he said, slapping me on the back. Then he put his big heavy arm around my shoulders and grew alarmingly serious. "I want to thank you, brother, for giving Melinda the secret text—that long-lost notebook from your grandfather's sea chest. It's 'the stuff that dreams are made on,' just like *The Maltese Falcon*."

"It's only a local legend," I protested.

"You know better, Dodge. That's why you revealed the book to her. I'm sure now that it was Fate that brought us together here in Croaker Neck, and I promise not to let you down."

For better or for worse, I had Shutterspeed on board. Now there was one last player to convince. And he would be the toughest by far.

I found Johnny at the harbor, leaning over the *Lady Ann's* transom to work on something below the waterline.

"Transducer came loose," he said, answering my too-obvious question. Cantilevered that way, hanging by the strength of his toes jammed up under the rail, it wouldn't have taken much of a mistake for him to fall overboard, wrench and all. I grabbed his ankles and held on until the job was finished.

"Damn, I'm too old for this." Johnny wiped his forehead with a rag, tossed it and the wrench into a bucket full of tools and rusted parts.

"Aw, come on. You're still spry."

"I'm still fat," he said, lighting up a Kool. "What are you here for, other than to complete a perfectly mommicked day?"

"How would you like to get some insurance against our little Raleigh adventure coming back to bite us? I've got an idea that could give us some cover. Just don't flip out and throw me overboard when you hear it, okay?" I told him my complete and well-rehearsed story about how the smartest thing he could ever do would be to take Ilse Brunner shrimping while Shutterspeed gets the whole lesson on videotape.

"When it makes the news that Johnny Bollard is trying to make peace with the turtle lovers . . . why, the SCC won't be able to touch you. If they try to start something, you can say they're singling you out, because you're a celebrity!"

Naturally, Johnny accused me of being out of my mind.

"A celebrity! Is that what you think I want to be? I'm just tryin' to make a living."

That's when I used my superior powers of persuasion.

"You won't reconsider?" I asked, trying not to sound too much like a car salesman.

"No way."

"Well, if that's the way you feel. You know, the TNN network is all hot to run something. Maybe CBS, too. So I need to find someone else."

"What do you mean, someone else?"

"Digger will do it." I hadn't asked him, but I still had E.V.'s three hundred-dollar bills, and for that kind of money Digger would take Al Sharpton shrimping.

"Digger!" Johnny flipped his cigarette butt overboard and began to stomp around on the *Lady Ann's* deck. "You can't put Digger on TV, people will think we're a bunch of psychos." He pronounced it *soy*-cose.

"Hey," I said, spreading my arms, palms toward Heaven. "It's your call."

"Jesus, Dodge! I get you a little extra money helpin' us out, and you let it go to your goddamn head!" He called me ungrateful, he called me conniving, he called me everything but a ham sandwich. But when he finally calmed down I had Johnny's agreement that he would take Ilse out for a short lesson in shrimping.

In my rush to close the deal with Johnny I'd nearly forgotten one minor detail: Ilse had made her going along conditional. Believing that my friend's resistance was pretty low, I sprung my last surprise.

"Uh, old buddy, you wouldn't have anything to do with planting that turtle in the Beaufort mayor's pickup, would you?"

"Hell, no!"

I reached for the cell phone lying on the helm.

"You won't mind telling Ilse that for me, will you?"

So far my plan was working just fine. Trusting Melinda had come naturally—and even if it turned out to be a mistake it was too late now. There was one more person I needed to see, to try and get a reading on just how sticky this particular mud flat might turn out to be. I'd been carrying his business card in my wallet long enough. It was time to call Special Agent in Charge Ron Gatlin.

chapter thirteen

We arranged to meet at The Velvet Elvis, a bar and grill in Beaufort with a set of decent pool tables.

Before going to the Elvis I walked down Ann Street, to the Old Burying Ground. The famous pirate Otway Burns is buried there, under an updated sarcophagus topped by an iron cannon. Of the many graves from the eighteenth century, the one I'm always drawn to is the single marker put up in memory of the crew and passengers who died on the *Crissie Wright*. Legends differ as to how many sets of remains are actually buried in Beaufort. Some say only the fat cook, who survived the cold night because of his girth and then died years later ashore. But the marker says all eight souls who were aboard the *Crissie Wright* lie there, and that's good enough for me.

My morbid visit was interrupted by the ringing of a bell. As the shrill sound filled the dozen blocks of the old town I recognized it as the signal that the drawbridge over Gallant's Channel was being raised. Life was going on, by land and by sea, and I walked out the iron gate to Ann Street, put my cap back on, and pointed its bill toward the Velvet Elvis, not knowing whether the NOAA agent would listen to my story or toss me in jail.

The Elvis is like a sore thumb in the Beaufort historical district. A brick-and-plate-glass storefront, it survives only because it was there long before Beaufort was taken over by the what the locals refer to as "the Hysterical Association." Inside I ordered a Bud draught and thought I was minding my own business, except I must have glanced one too many times at the old Brunswick pool table nearest the back, where a skinny guy in cutoff jeans, deck shoes, and a stained T-shirt was lazily running his way through a rack of balls. On the back of his T-shirt was the Calcutta Baits skull and crossbones ("Best Baits You'll Ever Drag"). I'd seen him before, in Beaufort bars and around the waterfront. His name was Mose, like the blues singer, and he worked as a fill-in mate on charterboats. Other times he could be seen grinding bottom paint in one of the yards. The Elvis served as a sort of hiring hall for an assorted crew who lived on small sailboats in the creek or shotgun shacks in the not-yet gentrified districts of town.

"Game of eight-ball?" he asked me, without looking up.

"Sure." I wasn't afraid of getting hustled. It was too early and I was too sober. "You want to flip a coin, see who breaks?"

"You go ahead," Mose said. "I have better luck if I don't break the first rack. You know, if I was any luckier, I'd have to be twins." He was one of those guys who wanted to do all the talking, which was fine with me. I concentrate better when I don't have to talk.

"Seriously. You know what they say? That I've got a horseshoe up my ass. That might sound painful, or even perverted, but all it really means is that I am one lucky sumbitch. Always have been, hope I always will be."

I broke, making not a thing. I re-chalked the crooked house

stick I was holding and said that maybe I was taking too big a chance, playing with the likes of him.

"Naw, not you. I can see you got a game. Watch me shave that three-ball right in the side." And he made it, got good shape on the seven. After a run of five balls he missed on the eight, leaving me a half dozen stripes to shoot and the cue ball frozen against the end rail. I made a couple of shots before he finally asked me where I came from.

"Croaker Neck? Lots of trouble there lately."

"What kind of trouble are you talking about?"

"Shrimper trouble. Turtle trouble. Did you hear about the latest?"

I hadn't.

"Two days ago, that guy that bought Murdock's Island had his car disappeared from where he left it parked outside the marina on Harkers Island. It was a brand new BMW and he'd left it there and gone off with some lady realtor from Salter Path. Mr. Tycoon, Cruz, I think his name is, comes back the next morning, his BMW's gone, and he starts pitching a fit right there in the parking lot, cussing everybody out for standing around laughing at him.

"Finally he calls the Sheriff, a deputy comes over and makes his report. Asks around, but nobody's seen nothin'. The deputy's kind of suspicious, because as far as he knows there's never been a vehicle theft on Harkers Island. It's just like Croaker Neck, people leave their keys in the cars and their boats and their front doors unlocked all the time." Mose looked at me, his eyes twinkling.

"They even leave the keys in their forklifts sometimes."

"Forklifts?"

"So, the deputy takes down the information, puts it out on

the computer, all that stuff." He stopped talking, wanting me to coax the rest of the story out of him.

"So, did they find the BMW?"

"They found it, all right. At the top of the dry stack." The dry stack on Harkers Island is a big blue metal barn where boats are stored on metal racks that reach three stories high. Boats as long as twenty-five feet are snatched out of the marina by a very large forklift and deposited in the racks. It takes great care and skill to do the job without scratching fiberglass or dinging prop blades, but Ricky, the lift operator at Harkers Island, seems to know his job.

"Ricky goes in the barn with the lift three days after the fancy car's gone missing. He was on his way to the last bay, way in the back, all the way on top, to pick up some weekend warrior's Aquasport, and notices that instead of seeing a keel and cavitation plate he's lookin' up at four tires and a chassis. Ronnie goes and gets old crazy Joe the outboard mechanic, and Joe climbs aboard the forks. Ronnie goes back in the seat and lifts Joe up there toward the ceiling and he reports down that it's a dark blue BMW seven-something, all right."

"Damn," I said, "I'd like to see that."

"Well," the mate said, "it's probably one of your neighbors that done it. Don't you think?" He came over like he was going to whisper in my ear, pausing to use his shirttail to wipe up the sweat ring my draught had dripped onto the table's wooden rail. I noticed that the wood was at least fifty years old and scarred by cigarette burns and so many coasterless beers that the felt appeared to be surrounded by a hundred interlocked sets of Olympic rings. "Come on, Dodge, people like you and me know it was them hard crabs from Croaker Neck that put a purse seine around them cars up in Raleigh."

How'd he know my name?

"Twelve ball in this corner," I said, "once back." I made the shot, and started to wonder what the guy's game really was. I wanted to get away from him, but there was still no sign of the NOAA agent.

"What brings you to the county seat?" The guy alternated between too much bullshit and too many questions. When I told him I was meeting someone he nodded, then stuck out his hand for me to shake.

"My name's Mose."

"Yeah, I've seen you around. I'm Dodge."

"I know. Let me give you a nice tight rack, here."

I broke and made nothing—the rack had been loose as a goose. Mose called his shot and missed. I made three low balls before he distracted me again.

"Looky there," he said in a lowered voice, nodding in the direction of the large Black man coming through the door. Gatlin was out of uniform, and the tan silk T-shirt stretched over his torso made him look even more lethal than his regular blue jacket. He was carrying his own two-piece cue in a lizard- or snake-skin case under his arm, and stopped at the bar long enough to get his own draught beer before walking over to our pool table.

"The bartender says you play nine-ball." He was talking to Mose, and already screwing his stick together. It looked like bird's-eye maple with the ivory from half an elephant tusk stuck in the base.

"I'm normally more of an eight-ball man myself," Mose mumbled, "but I ain't prejudiced." The cop gave the mate a funny look, then they agreed to play a race to seven for twenty dollars. Finally acknowledging my existence, he said, "Howdy, Lawson."

Gatlin was not a small man, but his hands were even bigger than his body called for. When I shook with him, my own hand disappeared like it was inside a catcher's mitt, and when he spread his fingers in a bridge to break that first rack, it seemed to fill up one end of the table. He drew back, snapped the cue forward, and nine balls jumped up and scattered for the rails like they were looking for a place to hide. But he'd juiced it a little too much, and the cue ball came off the table. Mose, ball in hand, said to Gatlin, "Dodge here is from Croaker Neck. And that's about as much as he's told me all afternoon."

"I know all about Mr. Lawson here." Mose, who was about to shoot, looked up quizzically.

"If you know him, then why—?"

"I thought he might tell you things he wouldn't tell me." He'd sent Mose in to soften me up, or trip me up. Any hopes I'd had of tricking the NOAA agent into giving *me* information flew out the door. As Mose played on against Gatlin I realized I'd been set up in more ways than one. The way he kept making shot after shot, and looking up at me in between each downed ball, he'd obviously been a sandbagger from the start.

Finally I said to the agent, "Can you and I talk, without your partner?"

"What do you want to talk about?" Gatlin asked. "I know. Let's start with monkey-wrenching?"

"What the hell's monkey-wrenching?" asked Mose.

"You tell him about it, Lawson."

"A monkey-wrencher is someone who fights against progress. You know, like throwing a monkey wrench into the gears? A writer made it up."

"*The Monkey Wrench Gang*," Gatlin said. "Edward Abbey, right Lawson?" He was sort of leaning on his cue and looking at me with a tilted head. "This piss-ant writer believed that it was a monkey-wrencher's duty to break the law in service to a higher law. Environmental do-goodism taken to an extreme. A criminal extreme. What I can't figure out is how that law-abiding commercial fishing crowd puts up with it."

"Maybe they're in on it," Mose suggested. They'd both stopped shooting and were looking at me. I had become the meat in a sandwich that was one slice of white bread and one of pumpernickel. As if on cue they stopped the staring routine and Mose bent over the table, racking, while the agent went to the hand chalk. The whole ball of talc disappeared into his paw. He turned back to the table brushing his palms together, the way you do after finishing a job of work. "Mose, let Dodge here rack. You go on home." As he left I wondered what they had used to squeeze him into turning informant.

"Let's you and me shoot a game," Gatlin suggested. Not seeing that I had much choice, I broke, made the one ball but left myself in a bind on the deuce. Got lucky enough to bump it and leave the cue ball all the way at the opposite end of the table.

"A whole lotta lawn to mow," he said, then he let out all his air in the deepest of sighs and struck that white ball so it hit the blue ball perfect, caroming it off the near cushion and across into the opposite side pocket. Then he ran the game out.

"Purty work," I said.

He calmly took his stick and started fooling around, making random bank shots until finally asking me, "Is there something you wanted?"

Nothing else in the Velvet Elvis stirred except for the ceiling fans. Even the bartender had gone off somewhere.

"I've set it up so Johnny Bollard and Ilse Brunner are going shrimping together."

"That's nice. But what's that got to do with endangered species violations?"

"Well, uh, Ilse wouldn't go near anyone she suspected of harming turtles. Doesn't that mean something?"

"It doesn't mean squat, not to me. What *would* mean something is if you can tell me who's hijacking turtles and planting them in Jacuzzis and koi ponds and God knows where next."

"That I don't know."

"But you will, Lawson. And when you do you're going to tell me, right?"

Gatlin took aim at a ball, then he broke out of his shooting crouch, stood with the base of his cue on the floor, and looked at me across the corner of the table.

"I used to hustle this game, you know. Played so well that it was hard for me to find a money game anywhere in the state, unless I gave so much weight that I didn't stand a chance. But I don't enjoy shooting pool for money anymore. I just like going to poolrooms. Always have, even when my mama would wear out a switch on my ass if she heard about it. You come in here, it's so quiet, nothing but chalk squeaking on cork and the sound of the balls."

I was staring at my shoes when he draped his arm across my neck, and laid that big dark hand of his on my shoulder, just resting it there. Still looking down, I closed my eyes.

"There's one man in Croaker Neck who knows everything that's going on," Gatlin said evenly, "and that's Johnny Bollard. Tell him that if his conscience should get to bothering him, he ought to give me a call. In the meantime the both of you need to steer clear of any more monkey business. Especially if it involves anyone in Raleigh."

I opened my eyes again, and the heavy paw came off my

shoulder. Then Gatlin moved to unscrew his cue. The motion reminded me of a doctor meticulously disassembling some long and unpleasant probe. But he wasn't quite finished.

"What do you know about your buddy Shutterspeed?"

"Not much." Which was the truth. "He's a friendly whacko."

"He ever ask you for money?"

"No."

Gatlin didn't react to that, he just finished taking apart his stick. When he'd put both pieces of maple in the snakeskin case he looked at me, and the light caught him just such a way that he had a look of weariness on his face, as if he'd been doing hard physical work for an awful long time.

"Did old Mose tell you about the horseshoe that's supposed to be up his ass?"

"He did."

"Well, maybe it's you that's got the horseshoe," he said as he headed out the door. "Go on back to Croaker Neck, and stay out of trouble. And let's hope I don't see you at any more freaky turtle rescues."

I went straight to the bar, ordered a fresh Bud, and brought it to my lips with a hand that was shaking so bad I nearly chipped a front tooth. Then, through the dirty storefront window, I noticed Digger on the sidewalk across the street. He was leaning against the side of his Powerwagon like he'd been there for a while. His visor cap was pulled down low but he was obviously looking toward the Elvis, where he couldn't have missed seeing me shooting pool with Gatlin—or missed picking up that Gatlin was a cop. I hopped off my stool to catch him, but by the time I reached the front door the tailgate of his truck was rounding the corner onto Front Street.

chapter fourteen

As the sailing time for his peace-making voyage, Johnny Bollard chose midnight, knowing that the other boats would have left the harbor long before—just to make damn sure none of his friends would see the head of Tortugas Now! climbing on board the *Lady Ann*.

Ilse was right on time, and he greeted her pleasantly enough, no "Turtle Nazi" or any of that. Shutterspeed and Pogy showed up, each lugging a case full of camera gear. A thunderstorm had blown through earlier and the last remnants could be seen lighting up dark clouds off to the northeast. Back to the west, the sky behind the squall line was clear and filled with stars.

Motoring into Core Sound, we found the water slick, the Banks a mile away faint in the waning moonlight. To the northeast a trail of bright lights—the cockpit lights of boats just like Johnny's—showed from one edge of the sound to the other. When the gear was ready the *Lady Ann* would be joining the conga line of dancing lights. After the rain the night had turned cool, and everyone but Pogy slipped on an extra layer of clothing.

From behind us the lighthouse beam reflected off of Ilse's slicker as it swept by every fifteen seconds.

Johnny turned his helm over to Pogy so he could walk aft and show Ilse the turtle excluders. The TED is pretty simple, nothing more than a round metal grid sewn into the funnel-shaped net. As the nets are dragged along the bottom, shrimp and small fish pass through the TEDs and into the tail of the net, the narrow bag at the end of the funnel where the catch is collected. Sea turtles, sharks, and fish too large to get through the TEDs are deflected out an escape hatch.

"What do you say let's drag," Johnny said. Shutterspeed shouldered his camera and began to roll.

Working in the flood of light put out by two quartz halogen fixtures in the rigging, he carefully tied slipknots in the tail bag to secure the catch. Then he threw the trawl net over the rail. The tickler chain clanked as it ran off and then the wooden doors sailed overhead and splashed into the ocean. When the towlines came taut the mast of the *Lady Ann* creaked and her engines idled up under the strain.

We dragged back and forth and up the sound for a while, then Johnny worked the levers at the base of his mast and soon the doors came back over the rail, followed by the floats of the trawl. Then the net was hoisted above the culling tray, and Johnny broke loose the slip knots he had tied and emptied our catch onto the tray below. There was a mountain of shrimp, plus the bycatch—small croakers, flounder, and other fin fish too small for the TEDs to exclude.

Ilse quizzed Johnny about the "little fishes."

"Up until '76, we used to be able to sell the bycatch. The Magnuson Act put a stop to that. So if we can't sell it, then why would we want to catch it, even by accident? It's just more junk to cull. I always throw what's alive back in the water as soon as I can."

Ilse nodded, while Shutterspeed continued to roll tape.

"When my daddy started shrimping back in the '50s, there were a lot more shrimpers, and they caught around seven million pounds a year. Now there's not half as many boats, and last year we took ten million pounds, just in North Carolina."

When we were away from the others, Ilse asked me how Johnny could reel off facts and figures like that.

"All these guys know that stuff," I explained. "They learn it when they're kids."

We towed toward Drum Inlet, passing the lights of Davis and Sea Level and Atlantic on the mainland shore. Johnny talked on the radio to other boats, and we heard rock music blaring from some of them. Over against the Banks we could see flounder giggers with their own sets of lights protruding from their skiff bows at an angle that nearly touched the water. Finally we turned and zig-zagged back down Core Sound toward Harkers Island. But the interesting part was over, and what remained was just work. In his cabin, Johnny showed Ilse how to make an easy chair out of life jackets. It didn't take much encouragement to convince her to curl up there and nap as the *Lady Ann* worked her way back toward the winking beacon on the horizon. When the doors came on board for the last time my tide watch showed incoming water and sunrise less than an hour away. The worklights went out and we could see the stars overhead and the bright lights of the state port toward the west. Ilse stepped to the rail beside me.

"What do you think?" I asked.

"I don't know. I can't believe that everybody is as good at this as Johnny."

"Maybe not. There are bad apples in any job. But maybe you could try seeing things his way. If you go to court with the SCC, you could wipe out a hundred families like Johnny's, just in Carteret County."

When we came close to Shell Point, at the east end of Harkers Island, we could see a train of bobbing red-and-green lights, paired close together and stretching down Back Sound, off toward Beaufort.

"What in the hell is that?" Shutterspeed asked.

"That," answered Johnny, "is boys and their toys. The checkout station for this weekend's king mackerel tournament is right here at the marina."

"Those are all boats?" Ilse said, not believing.

"Yep. Close to six hundred. That's what the Pit Cookin' Classic gets every year, isn't it, Dodge?"

Yes, every pair of bobbing red-and-green eyes was the set of running lights on the bow of a fishing team's boat, waiting for daylight and the official starter's pistol. Sponsored by a fast-food chain based in Rocky Mount, the Pit Cookin' Classic is the biggest of the seventy-two official king mackerel tournaments held in the Southeast every year. As parties go, the Classic is right up there with Spring Break—only the frat boys are thirty years older, sixty pounds heavier, and they have way more money for beer and other goodies.

The marina dock that would serve as the starter's platform was lit up like Times Square, and in that glare we could see a thickening haze of two-stroke exhaust on the water, the output of close to a thousand Yamahas, Suzukis, Evinrudes, and Mercs.

(Most king-chasing boats have two motors, but some have three.)
Every team had paid the $500 entry fee, plus $500 or more for
side bets. They had filled their bait well with live shad—at $10 a
dozen—punched destination numbers into their GPS devices,
iced their beer, double-bagged their sandwiches, and here they
were, sitting on "Go."

Johnny threw the *Lady Ann* into neutral and turned to Ilse.
"You want to watch?"

"You don't want to miss this," I said, knowing that our captain
had been planning to put us in this exact vantage point from the
minute he'd insisted on holding Ilse's shrimping lesson on Friday
night.

He'd gone along because he had a plan that trumped my
sorry conspiracy all to hell. Compared to Johnny, I was no
schemer at all.

The tide was nearly slack and we drifted slowly toward the
main channel on the last of the incoming. The idling motors of
the tournament fleet were like vague whispers in the dark, and
we could hear VHF radios crackling with static, the shouts
between boats too distant to comprehend.

In the light of false dawn the Core Banks began to take shape,
gray and low behind us. Twenty miles east a bank of clouds over
the Gulf Stream was backlit by the rising sun. I knew that All
Hell would break loose when the tournament boats started
checking out, but as usual All Hell was keeping its own schedule.

The tinny buzzing of a small outboard motor cut through
the throaty idling of the tournament boats. It was joined by a
second one, like bees approaching in the dark. When the noise
got closer the light of a reluctant dawn revealed two oddly built-
up inflatable dinghies traveling for us at top speed. The two
were identical, both done up in lime green papier-mâché, the

outlines of scales, dorsal fins and pectorals, an eye on either side: floating parade floats in the shape of giant green fish.

At the last minute the first dinghy pilot must have seen the shape of the *Lady Ann*. It turned sharply, the second boat following. When they cut the motors a hundred feet from the starter's dock, each paper dorsal fin opened like the lid on a tank, and up popped the occupant's head kissing a bull horn. A loud, electronic click was followed by a high voice, asking the over-amplified sheepish question, "Is this thing on?"

"Bull horns?"

"This oughta be fun," said Johnny, dropping anchor.

"What's going on?" Shutterspeed had dozed off; now he was struggling to get his camera out of its waterproof case.

"PETA," Johnny answered. He started to say something else, but that was drowned out by the noise of two bullhorn-assisted voices shouting, in a call-and-response alternation: "Fishing-hurts-fish! Fish-feel-pain!"

From the official Pit Cookin' dock, a third megaphone clicked on. Through a slip of the trigger finger, the first words of the morning from the official Pit Cookin' Classic tournament starter were the ever-popular, "Fucking assholes," followed by a loud throat clearing.

"The tournament starts in ninety seconds," the land-side voice warned. "Clear the starting area!"

The PETAns ignored him. Ninety seconds of "Fish feel pain!" passed before the starting gun fired. In rapid succession the boats in that long line went from idle speed to full throttle. A thousand outboards wound up and a thousand stainless steel variable-pitch, super high-performance propellers turned Back Sound into a very large and salty milkshake machine.

Seeing the wall of white water headed toward him, one of

the protestors immediately started his motor and turned tail. But just as he hit the throttle his stern went under, the motor drowned, and he was pooped. The second boat never made a move. It simply flipped upside down and spread a mat of green toilet paper on the water.

The force of the wake-froth carried the disabled dinghies towards us, and the two overboard PETAns at least had the wit to hold onto their floating statements. Johnny picked up a line and made a perfect toss. The first floundering survivor grabbed hold and we pulled him alongside.

As I was looking for a second line, Shutterspeed came rushing back from the bow to ask, "Why are we rescuing these morons?" Johnny didn't answer, he just looked at him with disgust and went back to keeping his eye on the second guy, who had foolishly abandoned his boat to swim toward his rescued buddy.

"Captain's responsibility," I explained to Shutterspeed. "Render assistance to any vessel in distress."

"Even during a mission?" The guy was definitely getting obsessed with this "mission" business.

Predictably, the second protestor began having problems swimming in the boat wakes. At his first cry for help a shape knifed into the water on the starboard side of our bow. Pogy brought the drowning fish-man to the rope alongside, then set off swimming for the overturned inflatable. He righted the craft, climbed in, and started fooling with the motor. Once he got it started he circled us, chanting, "Fish tastes good!" Then he went off to collect the second inflatable.

One of the tournament boats cut out of the starting grid and headed our way. The familiar thirty-one-foot Scarab idled to within hailing distance. Along the length of its hull was the name, *Vaporizer,* and Gus Ridge, the head of the SCC, stood at the center console. He and his fishing team were decked out in matching suits of yellow foul weather gear, their fancy raincoats covered in sponsors' patches, like a NASCAR pit crew.

Next to me, Ilse slipped out of sight.

"Hey, captain!" yelled Ridge. "You got some trash on board you want to get rid of?"

"Say again?" Johnny called.

"Is that Johnny Bollard?" Gus Ridge was trying to shield his eyes from the sun that was rising directly behind us.

"Yeah, Gus. Haven't seen you in a while. How you doin' this morning?"

"I'll be better if you give me those PETA peckerheads so I can wring their scrawny necks."

"Aren't you in the tournament today?" Johnny said. Relaxed, just making conversation. "If I was you, I might forget about these boys and get goin'. You don't want everybody beatin' you to the big prize."

"I got plenty of time," Ridge answered, making it sound like a threat. When Johnny didn't respond, Gus sharpened his tone. "C'mon, Bollard—you don't want to fuck with me. The Raleigh cops have got about a mile of net that I'd like to see wrapped around your neck. But maybe I'll forget about that, if you just toss those nutcakes back over the side where I can take care of them."

About that time a boat wake slapped the opposite side of the *Vaporizer* and three poorly secured hatches popped open—including the lid over the fish box built into the deck. In the box, on a bed of ice, was the unmistakable torpedo shape of a large king mackerel. The state's leading conservationist was clearly cheating his ass off, because checking out with a fish already on ice is a clear violation of the tournament rules. Considering that first prize in the Classic is over a hundred thousand dollars, it may even be a felony.

One of the crew slammed the lid, but too late.

"What's that you got in the box there, Gus?" Johnny called. "A little fishin' insurance?"

"Fuck you, Bollard," was the best the five-time champion could do, just as his *Vaporizer* drifted into the shadow cast by the much taller *Lady Ann*. With the sun out of their eyes, Gus and his two buddies could finally see us clearly: Johnny and I standing at the rail, and between us Shutterspeed with his camera aimed at them, point-blank. The sportsmen could do nothing but stare.

"Hey, Gus," Johnny yelled, "you want to hold that big king up, so we can make sure our cameraman here got it?"

This time Ridge had no witty replies. Using the butt of his fist he hammered down the throttle and followed the boat parade toward the ocean. After his wake stopped rocking us we lowered the PETAns into their defrocked dinghies and brought Pogy back aboard. The revived protestors set off for the shore, towing the wounded craft on a short length of Johnny's line.

He'd been cool with Ridge, but Johnny lost a little of that self-control now. Turning on Ilse, he blurted out, "You think that bastard really gives a damn about your turtles?"

She was quiet. Shaken a bit by what she'd just seen.

"Well? Are you going to court with Ridge, against *me*?"

"I think that you are tired," Ilse said weakly. "I know I am." She left the wheelhouse to go sit on a cooler of shrimp, where she stared at the *Lady Ann's* wake all the way home.

At the Croaker Neck dock we all parted in silence, except for Pogy and Shutterspeed, who couldn't stop cackling over their "mission" and the real Gus Ridge that had just gotten caught on tape.

chapter fifteen

I spent the morning dozing in the hammock on my porch. After waking in the early afternoon, I started adding up my personal score at the half-assed cloak-and-dagger game I'd been playing. My attempt to trade information with Gatlin had done nothing but make Digger so suspicious of me that he'd stopped answering his phone. The scheme that brought Johnny and Ilse together still might work out for the Seafood League, but after spending the night with her on the *Lady Ann*, my final, painful, conclusion was that I'd never get Ilse back. That I was making a fool of myself, and everyone in town knew it. Everyone in two towns, counting Beaufort.

"Give it up," I said out loud. The clattering branches of the fig tree seemed to agree. Yesterday's squall line—the one that had blown through before we went shrimping—was a harbinger of a change in the weather. The wind was forecast to clock around through half the compass as the first nor'easter of the year, the one they call "the mullet blow," formed off the coast. The weather station's robot voice called for thirty knots and gusty by midnight.

The sudden change from summer to fall brought with it a feeling of dread. Too many balls were still in the air, too many loose ends in my life had yet to finish unraveling.

Through the day the barometer kept falling like a stone, and the wind picked up as promised, but I didn't want to sit alone inside the cabin. Instead I added layers of clothing and sat in the rocker watching pine straw blow along the ground and pile up against the camellia bushes that Granddad had planted so long ago. When darkness came I was still on the screen porch.

A set of headlights pulled into my yard and two camo-painted doors on a Chevy van swung open. The headlights showed me Shutterspeed and Melinda running in my direction.

"Dodge! We need your boat!" I jumped up from my chair. Even if Shutterspeed was unstable I could see from the look in Melinda's eyes that something serious was happening. She had started to push her hair back and then her hand was frozen in mid-gesture, like she was holding down the top of her head, keeping it from coming off.

"There's a fire," she said, pointing toward the sound. I walked to the back of the cabin, where I could see the glow of a brush fire out on Murdock's Island.

"You're right," I said. "A fire." I was trying to figure out why a brush fire on a deserted island that was safely downwind had both of them in such a panic.

"Pogy's over there," Melinda shouted. Shutterspeed just nodded, beyond speech, his head bobbing up and down like a lunatic's.

Five minutes later I had the dock lines loose and the *Gannet* in gear. Once we got in the wide part of Ballast Creek the northeast wind caught us broadside. It was blowing twenty-five knots or so with nothing but the skinny strip of the Core Banks between us and the whole Atlantic Ocean. The mullet blow was on a rampage, fanning the flames that were eating the trees and brush on Murdock's Island.

Melinda stood next to me, inside. There wasn't enough room for Shutterspeed's bulk, and he filled the doorway behind us.

"What's Pogy doing over there anyway?"

"Digging," Melinda answered.

"He sleeps there sometimes," Speed interjected. "There's a shack, on the other side."

But I'd heard Melinda's answer, and Speed trying to answer another way.

"What do you mean, digging?"

"Will, are you going to tell him, or do I?"

"We uncovered a possible archeological site on Murdock's Island," he admitted.

"We?"

Melinda picked up the ball. "Pogy's been digging there for years. He found all sorts of artifacts . . . ."

"Is that what you were taking pictures of the day the patrol boat started chasing us?"

"Partly. Pogy found a lot more than trinkets." Before I could ask any more questions, he rushed to change the subject again.

"Won't they send a fire boat or something?"

"There isn't one. Besides, Oscar is out to clear this island anyway." Maybe the dingbatters hadn't noticed, but the work crews had been burning larger piles of slash every day. The smell of smoke had been in the air for a week; if anyone else in Croaker Neck smelled it tonight he would probably turn over and go back to sleep.

"Poor Pogy," Melinda moaned.

Ahead of us, a quarter of the island was afire, flames leaping into the air. The stacked-up chop on the sound water had a hellish glow on top, the white caps turning orange as they broke.

"He'll be okay," I said, but then I double-checked the throttle, making sure I was turning all the RPMs that were safe. My target was Oscar Cruz's temporary dock, where the Coke machine was still a brighter red than the fire.

"You need to go around," Shutterspeed said. "He'll be on the other side. The shack is in the woods."

"That's the lee side, it'll be awful hot." The sky downwind of the fire was in fact full of flaming embers, any one of which could land on the deck or on top of the wheelhouse. But I remembered the patch of beach and knew that's where I should be headed. Not far at all, unless you're in a hurry, in a slow-chugging research vessel.

We cleared the eastern point and went in as close as I dared. I told Shutterspeed to get ready to toss the anchor as soon as I got our bow pointed into the wind. When I was ready he gave the Danforth a fling and I ran forward to tie off the anchor line. It was a gamble between letting out enough scope to hold us without swinging so close to the island that we would ground the running gear, or worse, catch a falling ember.

The crackle of the fire was in our ears when the anchor line came taut. Shutterspeed went over the side and landed in water that was over his knees. I pointed my six-cell Maglight at the shore to help him find his way. The light fell on Pogy's empty skiff, tied to an old stake pushed down in the mud. Pogy's boat, but no Pogy.

Grabbing Melinda with a hand on either shoulder, I told her she needed to stay with the boat and hail anyone she could raise on VHF channel 16. Then I went over the side and started for the narrow strip of beach where her maniac boyfriend was waiting. As I waded ashore something in the flashlight beam caught my eye: a second line tied to the mooring stake. With the light I followed the length of nylon rope twenty feet out into the sound, where the other end was tied through a hole in the shell of a full-grown loggerhead turtle. In the fire's light, its shell glowed like an outsized orange floating on the water.

The beach was empty when I got there. Soaking my handkerchief in the sound water, I held it to my face and plunged into the blackened, smoldering brush where Shutterspeed had disappeared. I followed his lead through the area where the fire had already burned, weaving my way after him through charred live oak trunks and stands of sooty fetterbush.

A freak gust of wind cleared the smoke to reveal the shack just as the crackling, gobbling fire reached it. The hut was nothing more than an overgrown duck blind sitting four feet above the ground on stilts. The opening underneath created a tunnel for the super-heated wind, causing the puzzle of weathered boards to erupt in a fireball that singed my eyebrows and showered sparks in all directions. I watched helplessly as a shape appeared in the crude doorway, dark at first before it burst into a fiery crucifix that twisted slowly in a quarter-turn one direction, then the other. Then Pogy's body fell onto the blackened ground.

Shutterspeed started to run into the fireball and I tackled him. That knocked the breath out of me and I lay there for a few minutes, breathing the cooler air near the ground. When I finally rolled over the flames had used up all the fuel near the shack and moved on. Only the pilings remained flaming, with Shutterspeed kneeling in the embers trying to breathe life into Pogy's mouth.

I ran to the boat, where Melinda sobbed in the background while I used the *Gannet's* radio to talk to the Coast Guard. They had already dispatched one of their boats, and gotten the Sheriff's office on the phone. It was clear that Pogy had been dead before he fell. I didn't need the coroner's report to know that drawing a breath inside that fireball would kill instantly. Nor did it take a fire marshal to figure out that the fire started when the nor'easter fanned the embers in a slash pile that must have been smoldering unattended when the site crew had left work for the day.

I grabbed my first-aid kit and started back over the side, to see what I could do for the burns that Shutterspeed must have sustained patting out the flames that were still coming from Pogy's clothes when he got to him. But before I could get overboard Melinda clutched my arm.

"Do you have to tell them?"

"Tell who? What?"

"About the dig . . . the turtles?"

"Pogy's dead!" I shouted, hardly believing she could think about a coverup. "God dammit, Pogy's dead!"

Before I went back to the shack I had a job to do. Up to my knees in Core Sound, I stumbled past Pogy's skiff and followed the nylon line out into the water. Using my folding knife I cut the loggerhead loose from his illegal tether. He had the strength to swim away, just like they always do.

chapter sixteen

In most ways, the people of Croaker Neck are as plain as the mud flats where they tong their oysters. Yet they celebrate homecomings and holidays with a degree of flourish I've never seen anywhere else.

They spend time and money they can't afford to light up their houses and trailers for Christmas. They create elaborate front-yard displays for Halloween, with Wizard of Oz scarecrows sitting on bales of straw. At Easter, you'll see thousands of brightly colored eggshells hanging from crepe myrtles and budding fig trees and willows just leafing out. But my neighbors put their greatest creativity on display in the graveyard. In the town cemetery and the dozens of family plots that rest under oak trees beside the roads of East Carteret, the graves of fishermen and sailors are decorated with flowers sculpted into maritime shapes—elaborate floral anchors, shrimp trawlers with booms of carnations spread wide, or azalea cuttings formed in the shape of a nun buoy.

On the day of Pogy's funeral his grave was topped by a

faithful flower replica of a Core Sound sharpie, the shallow-draft vessel that was invented here in the eighteenth century. The florist got every detail right, down to the spritsail rig known as a "leg o' mutton."

Reverend Walker, a pastor well known to the church-going members of Pogy's family, would preach. Through his undertaking connections Digger had arranged for certain free services, and gotten a significant discount on the fine walnut casket we all chipped in to buy. My contribution was the $300 Ellis Vaughn had paid me.

Digger and I exchanged a few words at the service, but he was still staying clear, thinking there was something unholy going on between me and the Black cop he'd seen me with in town. His level of paranoia told me he still had plans to make an illegal, ill-advised harvest.

Before the service started Johnny and I stood in our black suits in a corner of the cemetery, talking about the weather. The strong north wind behind the storm had blown out the last trace of summer's humidity and ushered in the unmistakable air of fall. The shallow water in the marshes and the sound was cooling rapidly, a tropism that would send the mullet gathering into acre-sized schools. Soon the females would be fat with roe, and every falling tide would carry a wealth of shrimp out of the creeks.

"You boys done good," he said, when we'd worn out the weather as a subject. Even though everything I'd done to try and save Pogy had been futile, my friends were kind enough to treat me like a would-be hero.

"Almost anybody could have done better," I said. "Anybody who had a faster boat."

"Wouldn't have mattered," Johnny said, repeating the

consolation he'd been giving me since the morning after the fire.

Across the graveyard Ilse was talking to Shutterspeed and Melinda. Her red hair against the midnight blue dress was heartbreakingly beautiful. Speed looked very large and solemn in his own black suit, the white of his shirt showing at his neck, his hair a snowy white that matched the bandages on both hands.

Johnny lit up a cigarette and asked the obvious question, "What was Pogy doing on Murdock's Island?"

"Been trying to figure that out myself," I told him. "You got any ideas?"

Johnny shook his head. Telling anyone, even Johnny, about the "dig" on Murdock's Island wouldn't do any good. It wasn't a coverup, exactly, just a promise I'd made that fiery night while Melinda and I sat together on the *Gannet* waiting for the help that was already too late.

We were exhausted, our backs against the gunwale. I'd bandaged Shutterspeed the best I could but couldn't talk him into coming back to the boat with me.

"Pogy believed that he'd found white people's pottery," she told me. "Even white people's bones, right here on this island."

"What's Pogy know about bones?"

Melinda fell silent for a moment, letting the wind fill the hole in our conversation. Stalling. Finally she gave up.

"Will convinced him they were the Lost Colonists' bones. Maybe even Virginia Dare's bones."

"Jesus!"

She told me how, from their first meeting, she'd been curious about Pogy's necklace. She thought she could recognize a few of the shards as Iroquois. Proud that he'd attracted Melinda's interest, Pogy brought her and Speed over to Murdock's Island and showed them his anchorite's shack and some of the stuff he'd dug up over the years. The notebook from Granddad's sea chest—Shutterspeed's "secret text"—only confirmed what they already wanted to believe.

"You're a professional anthropologist. Couldn't you set them straight?"

She chewed into her lower lip.

"Don't tell me you believed it, too?"

"At first it seemed like it might be possible. Some of the artifacts that Pogy showed me didn't look like things a coastal Indian would have. When I read in your Granddad's notebooks about how the sand keeps shifting, I thought that maybe *he* had uncovered the real reason the Lost Colonists had vanished without a trace. For 400 years everyone had been looking for a moving target. Roanoke Island, Cedar Island, why not Murdock's Island? I got excited enough about the idea to send two of Pogy's pieces of bone to a professor friend in New York. A forensic anthropologist. As soon as I shipped them off I felt like a fool, but I had to know."

"And?"

"Dr. Chesterton said they were interesting, but DNA testing proved they were Native American and not English. Also, they were closer to two hundred, not four hundred, years old.

"But Will wouldn't believe me. He wouldn't believe a letter written by the head of the Columbia University anthropology department. I couldn't tell if he was that far gone in his fantasy, or whether he just wanted to save this island that badly."

"Save this island?"

"He said we could stop the development. That they couldn't pave over the resting place of Virginia Dare."

"Is he nuts?"

"Maybe. Maybe now he is."

"But you went along, to save Murdock's Island."

"Yes."

I had to think about that for a while. And wonder how any of us was going to live with the way our curious digging friend had died. But at that time, at least, I was convinced that Shutterspeed was the type who could live with anything.

I asked her why they were messing with the turtles.

"The first one, in the Jacuzzi, Pogy did that before Will and I even got to Croaker Neck. He was just playing a joke. Later on he told me he thought that it might bring you and Ilse back together."

Something smoke-cured and foul rose in the back of my throat, so that I had to stand up and spit over the side.

"What about the other turtles?" I asked, sliding back down to the deck.

"I'm afraid those were Will's idea. One day, while they were working on the studio, Pogy told Will the story of how he put the loggerhead in the Jacuzzi. The perversity of the whole thing was irresistible for Will. It appealed to his love for monkey-wrenching. Together they started devising more and better places to put turtles."

"And BMW's?"

"Yes, they hid the developer's car, too."

"And how did Pogy catch the turtles?"

"He had a way of calling them. Some special beat he would bang on the bottom of the boat. The old guy had some remarkable powers."

I had to admit that Melinda was right on that score. Right enough for me to keep her story to myself. At least for a while.

At the graveside, Reverend Walker cleared his throat. We gathered, some of us an unlikely audience for a man of God. But he was more than up to the task. Inspired by the first hint of winter's chill, the reverend began his preaching with the familiar story of the *Crissie Wright*.

"The night was cold, and the moon coming onto full. January 11, 1886, and the schooner *Crissie Wright* was eighty-four days out of Rio de Janeiro, with eight hundred tons of phosphate bound for New York. But the weather turned and she struck the shoals just off Shackleford Banks, caught in a winter storm that blew the mercury in Beaufort down to eight degrees.

"On that frigid night the whalers of Diamond City gathered and lit a fire on the beach, drawn there by the far-off voices of the *Crissie Wright's* crew carried to them on the wind. The sailors called pitifully toward shore from the rigging, where they had lashed themselves above the storm-driven surf. Unafraid of the crashing sea, the bravest of the Diamond City whalers took to their wooden pilot boats and began to row, pulling desperately to reach the foundering ship in time.

"Pulling on one of those oars was the great-grandfather of the gentleman we come today to remember, the man we all knew as Pogy. Like many in this town, our late friend came from Banker stock, people who were stern and loyal and God-fearing. Unfortunately, on that cold night the whalers with all their strength could not reach the foundering ship, and all hands were lost in the bitter cold sea.

"Today, once again, the Lord beckons us to come to His service after we have experienced a mighty storm. For everything around us is wet with our tears. He has called us to His ship of old whose ribs and planks are sawed from the timbers that were a cross on a hill. The decks are stained red from the blood that flowed from the Savior who hung upon it."

As the Reverend Walker preached I looked across toward the harbor. On the closest piling a brown pelican watched the water intently, waiting for the finger mullet to betray themselves with a flash of silver or a ripple of nervous water. Nearby a pair of gulls tugged at opposite ends of a menhaden that had washed up among the shoots of marsh grass near the marker at the harbor's entrance. The grass had turned from summer's green to a rich golden hue.

The preacher's words strode on. "Standing on the deck of this vessel is the Pilot of men's souls. He takes our hand as we step aboard and sail from the shore. The Pilot prepares his net of Grace, and casts it into the depths of man's sin. The Pilot walks to His wheel and sets the course for a light in the distance, which is the Kingdom of God."

As the good people of Croaker Neck listened with their heads bowed, I saw Ilse look up, too. Our eyes met, and she smiled, sadly, and mouthed the words, "See me later."

"Ladies and gentlemen," boomed Reverend Walker, "the Pilot of men's souls is willing to set a new course for each of us. He will guide us through the dark days and the shoals that could bring us to shipwreck. He shall truly guard His own until we cross the bar one last time. In the name of the Father, the Son, and the Holy Spirit, Amen."

chapter seventeen

A week after Pogy was laid to rest Melinda called and told me
that they were holding a memorial the next evening at the studio.
"Will has been editing day and night, to finish a rough cut of the
film as a tribute to Pogy. So I guess it will be a premiere of sorts."

"Not another wake?"

"It won't be that wild." The night after the funeral we had all
gathered on Ballast Creek with plenty to drink. Melinda had
put away her share of whiskey that night. And Ilse, too, was
overcome by that wave of emotion that typically comes at
weddings, christenings, and funerals. We'd had a few drinks
together and finally got around to what had gone wrong between
us. Or what might go right in the future. Summer was long gone
now, but she was beginning to thaw.

Digger had passed on my invitation to the wake. Melinda
couldn't say for sure if he would be at the movie premiere. After
the way he had avoided me at the funeral I wanted to get him
alone, to tell him that the Black cop was a NOAA Agent, not a
narc.

To further complicate things, Gatlin still wouldn't leave. He was still hanging around Beaufort, still riding with the Marine Patrol, still adding to Digger's paranoia quotient. I now realized how far ahead of me Gatlin had been, that the real culprits had been his prime suspects all along. The night of the fire I had cut loose any direct evidence he could use against Shutterspeed. Still, he must have been sure that Shutterspeed would trip himself up in due time.

The night of the premiere the sunset was spectacular, and the invited group was standing out back of the crab house at the edge of Core Sound silhouetted against the western light show.

"I wonder if those red streaks in the sky have anything to do with that tropical storm in the Bahamas?" Shutterspeed asked, his voice coming to me out of the near darkness.

"That storm's eight hundred miles away from here." Johnny's voice. The voice of authority. "And it won't get much closer. This time of year, they either hit Florida or go out to sea." Hearing my feet scuff in the broken shell walkway, he turned and was the first one to notice that Ilse was walking with me.

"Look here, everybody, it's Dodge." Heads rotated on red necks, and my friends stood there grinning like a bunch of half-bright monkeys at the sight of me with Ilse. Melinda corralled her immediately and the women went inside in search of wine. Nobody said anything for a minute or two, then Johnny smacked me on the back.

Shutterspeed, though, failed to make any gesture that my date with Ilse had registered. He was distracted by preparations for the premiere, or preview, and soon went into the studio to get his act together. The bandages had come off his hands, but the skin was still blistered and pink. And he still wore his black suit.

With the others inside, the Fowlers, Johnny, and I lapsed into normal Croaker Neck talk. About oysters, and about how the cold spell would make them fatten up. About the mullet fishing, and the start of duck season, only two weeks away. People had already started to get their blinds ready, even though the early season wasn't usually very productive. Through it all Pogy's presence hung over us like Spanish moss in a dead oak tree.

Shutterspeed appeared in the door and announced that he was ready. That was when Digger's pickup pulled into the yard. I went down off the porch to meet him, figuring that the showing could wait a minute or two.

I told Digger I was afraid he wasn't going to show up. And that there were some things we needed to get straight.

"I only came because of Pogy," he said. He'd been drinking, or smoking some Poison, or both.

"That Black guy you saw me with in Beaufort? He's not what you think."

"He's a cop. Maybe you're a cop now, too."

"That guy's a turtle cop. Endangered species enforcement."

"One cop's the same as another. But it won't matter now. I got it hid where nobody can find it. 'Specially not you." On "you" he jabbed a finger into my chest, and I knew he was drunk enough to start something, Pogy tribute or not.

"Dodge," Ilse called, "everyone is waiting for you. Oh, hello Digger. You two better come on inside now."

Even as lathered as he was, Digger's confusion at seeing Ilse there dispelled his anger. He went up the stairs, told her hello, and went inside like a good boy. I followed. Grabbing Melinda by the elbow, I asked her, "How is this movie, anyway?"

"I don't know. He wouldn't let me see any of it."

Ilse and I went inside and looked for seats. The only light was a TV monitor's glow, and by that faint light she picked out the last folding lawn chair. The familiar plastic milk crates were scattered here and there so I turned one over and sat on that. In Pogy's absence the orderliness that had prevailed when the studio was being used for shooting had given way to something else. Thick black electrical cables snaked off into the dark, where I could make out the angular forms of the stands, booms, and tripods that hovered like jungle beasts just outside the glow of the oversized monitor. Still, there was something exciting about sitting down to watch a movie surrounded by the gear that had been used to make it.

Shutterspeed got up from his own seat and stood next to the monitor, the ringmaster of his very own video circus.

"We are here tonight to honor and remember our great friend Pogy. Because he gave the last weeks of his life to the production of our film, *The Real Virginia Dare*, I thought it appropriate to show a very, very rough version. What you're about to see is just a part of the film that I have planned.

"You all know the story of the Lost Colony, an account that originated with its woeful governor—and Walter Raleigh's business partner—John White. What you don't know is that the generations of historians who have perpetuated that story have simply added layer upon layer to a coverup."

Here Shutterpseed wandered away from the monitor, and became his disembodied voice bouncing off the steel walls and concrete floor of the crab house studio. An image of Sir Walter Raleigh appeared on the screen, the familiar sixteenth-century engraving.

"Let's take a look at good old Walter Raleigh, courtier—some say lover—to Queen Elizabeth. He was in reality a very nasty bastard from the West Country who first rose to prominence doing the Crown's dirty work in Ireland. The man your state capitol is named for got his start slaughtering Irish peasants. Then he worked his way up to piracy.

"By stealing the loot the Spanish had already stolen in Mexico and Peru, Raleigh and his friend Sir Francis Drake hit upon a daring shortcut to untold wealth. By 1580 Drake and his pirate ships were preying on the galleon fleet as it rode the Gulf Stream from Havana to Cape Hatteras before turning across the Atlantic toward Spain. But to do the job right the English needed a port in the New World where they could re-supply. And that was the real purpose for which John White and his innocents were sent to these shores. In a classic example of history being written by the winners, the misbegotten adventure in cold-blooded piracy has been turned into a glorious, noble experiment, symbolized by a so-called Lost Colony, by an innocent baby girl named for a Virgin Queen! And it was Pogy, rest his soul, who revealed all this and more to me."

Shutterspeed paused and cleared his throat. His speech had stunned everyone in the dark room into utter silence.

"After that bit of background, I believe you are ready to preview my rough cut of *The Real Virginia Dare*. I'll warn you, its style is highly experimental."

As he spoke those words the image of Raleigh dissolved into a photo of a grinning and gap-toothed Pogy with his magic necklace around his neck, and then over that the title, *The Real Virginia Dare*. The studio was filled by the soundtrack, a haunting solo organ. In a series of long dissolves the photo and title were replaced by a series of watercolors—beautiful depictions of fish, flowers, animals and Indians were all from the hand of John

White, who was a better painter than navigator. The music combined with the watercolors slowly dissolving into one another set a hypnotic mood, and the spell continued as the drawings were gradually replaced by exquisitely framed shots of their real-life counterparts. Some of them I knew, like the sarvissberry bush that blooms when the shad run, and the yaupon, whose berries were used by the Indians to make a hophead tea.

There were shots of fish, too. Blues, mackerel, croakers, a jellyfish, and a starfish. When the camera zoomed in on a school of pogies flicking at the surface, I looked around the darkened room to see all eyes frozen to the screen. Even the hardened saltwater cowboys seemed to have discovered a new lens for viewing the stuff of their everyday lives. Then there was a shot of Pogy, standing in his skiff holding up the same Kemp's Ridley that was found in the Beaufort mayor's pickup. In Agent Gatlin's hands, that minute of film alone was enough to get Shutterspeed hauled into federal court. But there was more: Pogy swimming with turtles, and basking with one in a koi pond surrounded by finning goldfish.

Then the music subtly changed, cross-fading into an arrangement and a melody line that was much more modern, much darker. The images on the screen changed, too. An up-angle shot of the lighthouse at night made it look more sinister that I'd ever imagined it could. A baby wailed in its cradle as through some video process its skin became bright crimson. A thicket of brush and small trees trembled and then gave way as the lethal blade of a bulldozer tore through it and rushed at the camera. These images of chaos and destruction layered one on the other faster and faster until the eye could barely keep up. The music quickened its pulse, too, until the instruments that had been added to produce the cacophony were removed one by one leaving only an insistent drumbeat to accompany an entirely new tableau: Melinda, writhing naked at the edge of the surf line on a beach that had to be Shackleford, because now a pony watched from atop a grass-covered dune. Back and forth, from Melinda/Virginia to the pony, on and on, until, just when it was getting entirely too kinky, the pony became . . . Pogy, stripped to the waist and dancing a jig in the doorway of the shack on Murdock's Island, his magic necklace jangling around his neck.

"Jesus Christ!" In the dark I couldn't tell if the oath came from Digger or Johnny. It didn't matter. Whoever had said it was speaking for us all.

The mad drumming built in volume as Pogy's dance shifted into slow motion and ever so slowly dissolved into the image of Virginia Dare lying on the beach as still as death while the Atlantic Ocean washed over her naked body.

The screen faded to black. The darkness was as welcome as the sighting of land after a bad day at sea. The sound of solitary clapping began, from the general area where Melinda was sitting. That noise was hesitantly joined by more tentative approval from the ever-polite Ilse. *What the hell?*, the rest of us all thought at once, and everybody began to clap. It seemed the sane thing to do, so we tried to make a cheerful noise in the darkened crab house, where cheer and sanity were in short supply.

As the lights came up my arm was sore where Ilse had been digging her fingers into the bicep. Shutterspeed was slumped forward in a chair, his head in his baby-pink hands. We all walked by, said whatever words we could muster, and went our separate ways into the night.

chapter eighteen

Almost exactly twenty-four hours later my phone rang, and I hated it for waking me out of the sweetest dream I'd had in years. There was a redhead involved.

"Hey," said the voice at the other end. "It's Johnny." He was on his cell phone, probably on a boat, judging from the background noise. My watch said 10:45 and a falling tide at the inlet.

"You need something?" I mumbled. Johnny never used his cell phone just to say hello, especially if he was working.

"I'm draggin' for jumbo shrimp," he said, "up in the Pamlico, off Chainshot Island."

"And?"

"I been hearing some strange mess on the radio, man. Thought maybe you ought to hustle up to Cedar Island and meet the last ferry."

"What for?" Something moved in the bed behind me. The moonlight filtering through the hydrangea bush outside my window was enough to reveal the spread of red hair across the pillow next to mine. I thought about hanging up the phone, but after all, it was Johnny Bollard on the other end.

"Near as I can make it out from the radio traffic," his clear voice continued, "some guy started acting crazy on the last ferry back from Ocracoke."

"So?"

"Big guy with a ponytail and a video camera. Screaming about saving Virginia Dare."

"Damn!"

"What is it?" Ilse sat up, startled.

"Look," Johnny went on, "I just thought maybe you'd want to know about our favorite dingbatter goin' nuts on the ferry."

"Okay, I'll drive up there. Can you meet me?"

"I'm catchin' shrimp so long as this *toide* holds out, cap'n. Cold front's on its way tomorrow."

"I gotcha."

"Take the redhead with you," Johnny said.

"How did you know?"

"I went to the same movie you did, bud."

When I told her what was going on, Ilse didn't try to talk me out of going to Cedar Island. She wriggled into her clothes and went into the kitchen. When she came out to the truck with coffee I was throwing trash, tackle, and hand tools from the cab into the bed, trying to make room.

"Sorry," I said. "It's been a while since I had a reason to clean up." She leaned forward and kissed me softly on the lips, so I quit apologizing. We drank coffee and came awake going down the deserted highway through towns that at that hour weren't much more than a light in front of the post office and another hanging above the doors to the volunteer fire station.

We drove over the high bridge above the Indian ditch and I wondered again what Digger planned to do. Farther on was the wide section of grass and scrub that is part of the Cedar Island National Wildlife Refuge. The bed of the road there barely rises above sea level and the borrow ditches on either side hold enough water to float a good-sized boat. We passed a number of them tied up next to the highway, where the fishermen reach them by parking their trucks on the grassy shoulder and walking to work in a couple of steps.

"We weren't supposed to be doing this, you know."

"Doing what?" I couldn't tell if Ilse was teasing me or not.

"Any of this," she sighed. "I wasn't supposed to be in your bed . . . that *ahs*-hole Shutterspeed wasn't supposed to be getting us out of your bed. I am so mixed up."

I reached across the bench seat and squeezed her hand. The next few miles through the marsh were tranquil, but the scene at the ferry landing in Cedar Island was not so lovely.

The rotating red lights on top of an ambulance turned the docks, the gray clapboard snack bar, and the empty asphalt boarding lanes into some kind of weird outdoor disco. The rescue wagon was backed right up to the landing, and bright light poured through the open doors of the meat compartment to shine on the dark water trapped behind the ferry terminal's castle wall of a rock jetty. On top of the jumbled mossy stones a green navigation light blinked out of sync with the ambulance beacons.

Once inside the breakwater the 220-foot ferry *M/V Carteret* cut its motors and used its bow thrusters to turn completely around as the ferry dock crew walked deliberately out of the government-issue shed where they wait between boats. The crew looked natty and efficient in the pressed-and-pleated tan uniforms of the state ferry service, known proudly as "the North Carolina Navy."

A volunteer EMT came out of the snack bar and walked toward the ambulance, a cup of vending-machine coffee steaming in his hand. Word had spread, and a small crowd of excitement-starved Cedar Islanders had gathered shuffling and mumbling near the ticket-taker's booth. In contrast to the wildly spinning light show, no one seemed to be in much of a hurry.

Fall is the prime surf fishing season, so even on its last run of the evening the boat's vehicle deck was packed bumper-to-bumper with 4X4 trucks and SUVs from several states. Like a scene out of a porcupine boatlift, each truck was bristling with CB antennas and ten- and twelve-foot fishing rods sticking straight up from rod racks mounted in front of the grill.

A north breeze buffeted that weathery point, but it seemed that none of the fishermen had taken refuge inside the trucks or the ferry's passenger cabin. Dozens of men in camo parkas and fleece vests lined the rail of the raised observation deck with their collars turned up against the wind. From the bridge above them two crewmen next to the pilot house aimed high-powered spotlights at the stanchions along the slip, lighting the way as the dockside crew took the thick lines threaded through the hawse holes and looped them over the iron bollards on the landing. Two more members of the crew moved around inside the lighted passenger cabin.

Once the lines were snug the captain shut off the engines and the spotlights winked out. But instead of dropping the boarding ramp to begin the usual parade of vehicles off the ferry, the boat just sat there and the fishermen stood against the rail, their cigarettes glowing orange against the sky. A quick glance at my watch told me the *Carteret* had been on the sound for almost four hours to make a crossing that usually takes a little over two.

I asked a tan uniform what everybody was waiting for.

"The Sheriff."

"What happened?"

"Some fool dingbatter jumped off the ferry."

Behind me Ilse gasped.

"Did they fish him out?"

"I have no *oy*dea," the crewwoman said.

A thin, familiar voice called my name from the ferry. I could see Melinda waving at me through the black metal grating of the vehicle ramp turned up like a fence keeping the passengers and vehicles on board. Her face had the look of a long-suffering prison inmate. In the shadows behind her Agent Gatlin looked at me with professional distaste, but he kept his distance as I leaned as close as possible and asked Melinda what had happened.

"Will . . . he just . . . became insane."

"Did he jump off the ferry?"

She nodded. In shock, or close to it.

"He's still out there," she sobbed. "In the water." Gripping the dirty metal, she hung her face toward the deck, but then jerked her chin up at the *thwack-whack* of a helicopter coming in low off the Pamlico. We watched as the Coast Guard chopper hovered above a sandy field beside the ferry terminal parking lot before coming to rest next to a barn painted with a jolly invitation to "Go Horseback Riding! Gallop On the Beach! By the Day or By the Hour." Our hopes were erased when no one jumped out of the chopper with any sense of urgency. The rotors stopped turning and the jet engine noise was replaced by the sounds of the tourist-broke saddle horses raising hell inside the barn. Their braying seemed to me even more distressing than Melinda's tears.

Sirens were now wailing, too, from just around the last bend in the road. Three cars—two beige county, one silver-and-black Highway Patrol—sped up to the landing and stopped so close to me I had to jump back to avoid being clocked by a door as the cops got out.

The fishermen lining the ferry's rail began to point toward the jetty, where another boat was coming into port. From the top deck of the ferry a searchlight trained on Johnny's *Lady Ann*, catching a twisted pennant of bright colors hanging from the boom. The flag was actually an inside-out Hawaiian shirt—yellow and pink palm leaves printed in reverse, hanging down low enough to cover a human body's face and arms, all except for the pinkish hands that strained for the deck. The man who chased Virginia Dare was wrapped firmly in yards of trawl net, kept company in his dripping shroud by the writhing forms of live shrimp.

"Melinda, don't look." But it was too late; she'd seen Johnny's haul. Her slender fingers lost their grip on the metal grating and she started slumping towards the deck. Gatlin came out of the shadows and caught her just before she fell over.

The Coast Guardsmen from the helicopter, a Highway Patrolman, and one of the Sheriff's men boarded the *Lady Ann* while the rest of the cops hustled up to the ferry pilot house to get the full story from the captain.

Johnny lowered the boom with its strange load down over the dock, where two deputies cut Shutterspeed's body from the net and wrapped him in a government-issue gray wool blanket. Ilse walked up behind me just in time to see one of the cops trying to stuff a long white ponytail back inside an end of the blanket roll.

"My God," she said, and brought her hand to her mouth. I put my arm around her. But then, as Johnny walked up, she shook loose and collected herself.

"Would you go get us some coffee? I've got something I want to say to your friend." It reminded me of the day years before, when she had, in effect, commanded me to buy her a fish at the fish house.

When I got back with the coffee, Ilse had finished her business with Johnny and gone back to my truck.

"Some catch tonight," he said, lighting up a Kool. We stood and watched the last of the fishermen's trucks start up and drive off into the night.

"What did she want to tell you?"

"That your trick may have worked. She called it *our* trick. I think she meant taking her out on my boat. Anyway, she's not going to court with Ridge and the SCC after all. Something about owing it to Pogy. What the hell made the big dingbatter jump like that, anyway?"

"I think maybe he blamed himself for getting Pogy killed."

"Did he? Get him killed?"

"Not that I know of," I said. But that didn't sound convincing, so, while the ferry unloaded, I told Johnny about the bones on Murdock's Island, the shack, and the turtles with holes drilled in their shells.

"Well, I'll be damned," he said when I'd gotten to the end. He absorbed the story, then gave Shutterspeed a grudging absolution. Call it a Croaker Neck version of the last rites.

"I'm not glad he killed himself, but it's good to know he had that much of a conscience."

"Surprised?"

"Hell, yes." In Johnny's system there was something right, some balance restored, in the way Speed dealt with his implacable burden, the fundamental, final way he'd wiped his own slate clean.

I had one thing I still needed to ask Johnny.

"Shouldn't Shutterspeed have gone out through the turtle shooter?"

"He would have except that his ponytail caught on the metal. Turtles, you know, don't have ponytails."

When the only vehicle left on board was a camo Chevy van I told Johnny good night and walked toward the ferry. I knew the Sheriff would probably hold onto Speed's van for a while, and that there was a frightened young woman in the passenger cabin who would need a ride back to Croaker Neck. The first deputy I saw didn't want to let me on board, but then Gatlin came out of the passenger cabin with his hat in his big hand and motioned for me to come on across the ramp. The deputy didn't seem to be happy about being corrected that way, by a cop not fitting the standard profile, but the Black NOAA agent was obviously large and in charge.

"How is it you just happen to be here, Lawson?"

I told him about the cell phone call from Johnny, and asked him the same question he'd asked me.

"I was bird-dogging your crazy pal."

"Why? He do something wrong?"

He very deliberately used both hands to re-tilt his hat on his head, saying that he wasn't going to be bullshitting around with the likes of me.

"Look," I said, "Don't you think tailing a guy and his girlfriend all over two counties is a little bit heavy? All Shutterspeed ever did was pull a few pranks. Maybe flirt with an ESA violation."

"Flirt?" He spat out the word. "There's two men dead because of his flirting."

chapter nineteen

When I came back to the truck with Melinda, Ilse quickly opened the door and made room for her in the middle of the bench seat. By that time her shock had worn off and a gabby sort of fatigue had set in. She needed to talk, and on the road home we heard the story of Shutterspeed's last squally evening on the planet.

The morning after the botched premiere Shutterspeed surprised Melinda by waking her up with a pot of hot coffee and donuts he'd brought back from the minimart. The black suit he'd worn since the funeral was gone, replaced by one of his flamboyant Hawaiian shirts. He was eager to follow through on a trip they had been planning, to Ocracoke.

"Let's go for a ferry ride," he'd said. "Just the two of us." Happy to see him snapped out of his extended mourning, she willingly went along.

They had an uneventful ride over to Ocracoke, where they walked on the beach until they found a stretch that hadn't been claimed by any fishermen. If the morning's coffee and donuts had been a surprise, they were nothing compared to Shutterspeed's insisting that they "do it" right there in the dunes.

"We made love," Melinda said, "the way we used to. Will was a passionate man, but for a long time he'd put it all into his movie. Today . . . Oh, God!" She stopped cold. "He was saying good-bye. He had it all planned!"

Recovering her composure, Melinda told us how, after their tryst in the dunes, they drove to Howard's Pub and drank a toast to Pogy. Shutterspeed may have had many toasts. While Melinda used the pay phone to make a reservation on the last ferry back to Cedar Island, she watched him start a conversation with a woman on the next bar stool. A golden retriever was lying on the floor between their stools, and Shutterspeed took a saucer from the bar and put it down next to the dog's big gingerbread head. The woman was laughing and she jangled five inches of turquoise bracelets in Shutterspeed's face like she was trying to hypnotize him.

When Melinda appeared the laughing woman told him that Speed had just bought her dog a drink. A double bourbon.

"Do you know who this is?" Shutterspeed asked his new companion.

"If it's your wife or your girlfriend, I ain't into that kind of stuff." The woman was obviously a regular; she was wasted and her dog was working on getting that way.

"She doesn't remind you of anyone?" Shutterspeed persisted. "Maybe . . . Virginia Dare?"

The woman responded by cackling and jingling her bracelets. The liquor and all the action in the dunes were catching up with her, and Melinda started desperately coaxing Will to get out of the bar and onto the ferry. By the time she succeeded the last boat was nearly finished loading. The camo-painted Chevy van was the final vehicle to board the *M/V Carteret*. As the lumbering boat slowly backed out into Silver Lake the two of them stood on deck and watched until the lights of Ocracoke had faded over the horizon.

On the Feast of the Annunciation, in 1524, Giovanni Da Verrazzano looked across a narrow spot on the Outer Banks and had no doubts that the endless body of water he saw on the other side was "the eastern sea." It wasn't the Pacific, of course, only the Pamlico Sound. But nearly five centuries later that shallow inland sea can still feel as large and empty as any ocean, especially at night. Even the blinking red-and-green lights on the channel markers are miles apart in some places.

In one of those lightless stretches Melinda woke from a short nap in the driver's seat of the van and saw Shutterspeed standing on the hood of a nearby Suburban, kicking out at the crowd of passengers. By the time Melinda slipped out of the van a uniformed crewman had joined the ruckus.

"The owner of the truck and his friends were going crazy because Will was denting the hood and whacking their fishing poles. He kept calling them rotten Spanish freebooters and much worse. I shouted Will's name and he looked me in the face. His eyes were glazed—a haunted look I'd never seen before."

When the crewman climbed up on the vehicle to collar him, Shutterspeed shoved him off and hopped from the Suburban onto another truck, then another, this one parked against the rail. Then, without a last look back, he dove over the side.

The crewman instantly threw lifesaving rings over the side. Two more pulled on life jackets and jumped overboard, even before the boat had stopped moving. By this time every passenger on board was along the rail. The fishermen called out and pointed into the blackness. Except for the captain and crew everything was bedlam.

Searchlights on the top deck were switched on and played across the water, after a few sweeps locking onto a white shock of hair bobbing a hundred feet behind the stern. The two crewmen in the water swam with everything they had. Another ring buoy was thrown, but it landed only halfway to the target. A target that made no effort to swim toward his rescuers. Finally, while everyone including Melinda watched helplessly, the white topknot slowly sank in Verrazzano's eastern sea.

"Will was a strong swimmer," Melinda told us. "He just didn't want to live."

"I'm sure you did everything you could," Ilse said soothingly. It was the first time she'd spoken on the long, depressing drive back to Croaker Neck. Melinda thanked her, then began to weep softly once again.

Back at Ballast Creek Melinda sat wrapped in a blanket in her favorite spot, up against Granddad's sea chest. Ilse brought her a cup of tea laced with brandy.

"What made him go off like that?" I asked.

"He was a genius, of course." Melinda seemed to think that explained something. "When I first met him in New York he came across as bigger than life. And he came along at a perfect time. I'd just lost a shot at a fellowship, and a dig in Egypt, because I wouldn't help the professor cheat on his wife. So I was ready to get out of town."

She sipped her tea, then repeated, "Will *was* a genius, you know! When I first met him he was obsessed with filmmaking. And with Virginia Dare. Maybe it's too much for one man to have two obsessions."

"Shutterspeed had three," I said.

"Meaning?"

"I think he was nuts about you. I mean, nuts in a good way."

"It was all so complicated," she said, as Ilse poured another shot of brandy into her mug. "At first I was nuts about him. So much that I didn't suspect a thing when he asked to borrow money for his film. 'An investment opportunity,' he called it. Then he had me put some equipment rentals on my credit card. Alarm bells should have gone off, but by then it was too late. I believed in his Lost Colony scheme. I *wanted* to play the grown-up Virginia Dare. He'd sold me on his whole crazy vision, just like the others."

"Others?"

"It took me a while to find out about them. I overheard a couple of phone calls. There were a number of overnight packages from an attorney's office in Brooklyn that he refused to open."

"So Gatlin wasn't the only one after Shutterspeed?"

"Three years ago, Will created a lot of hype around the Virginia Dare story as a feature film. He dropped the right names in the right midtown bars and without trying very hard he got three dot-com millionaires in their twenties to give him a hundred and fifty thousand dollars each."

"A hundred and fifty thousand!"

"It's not so much," Ilse said. "Not in New York."

"Especially not for Will," Melinda continued. "He was convinced the original three geeks could lead him to even more investors, but to tap into that he needed to look like a successful big-time filmmaker. He bought the Chevy van, and I bet he blew twenty thousand just buying clothes at Barney's."

"How did you find out about all of this?"

"Well, I was there for the end of the parties and the last of the shopping sprees." She lifted her leg and pointed a shoe towards Ilse for her inspection.

"You like these?" she asked. "Will bought them for me at Saks." The leather was crusted white around the edges from saltwater.

"We rented the equipment on my card our last day in New York. He said it was a temporary problem. Claimed he'd forgotten to move money between accounts. Then he asked me to drive out to Long Island City and pick up the rental equipment alone. I'm pretty sure he owed them money."

"Oh," Ilse sighed. "You poor thing."

"You know, people who make movies do that sort of thing all the time. There's this feeling of moral superiority. Of the artist against the world.

"When I found out Will was using me . . . I should have packed up my credit cards and run. But I'd bought in and I wasn't ready to cut out. He needed me too much."

And that was it. Melinda began to weep again and within a few minutes the brandy and exhaustion took hold. Ilse tucked her in on the couch and went off to bed herself.

Down at Granddad's dock the *Gannet* seemed content at the ends of her dock lines. There was barely a ripple on Ballast Creek as I sat on the worn planking and watched the sun come up. When there was enough light to read, I took an envelope out of my pocket. The return address read Columbia University.

Melinda had given me the letter, saying it was something that Pogy had left behind.

"His legacy," she called it.

Dear Melinda,

After our recent correspondence I took the liberty of contacting a Mr. Whitacre in the North Carolina Office of State Archeology, Department of History and Archives. I believe that your "source" gave you the impression that he had found "white people's bones mixed in with the Indians'." As I informed you earlier, there is little hope that the "white people's bones" were those of the Lost Colonists of 1587. DNA testing has shown all of the samples you provided from the Murdock's Island site to be of Native American origin.

However, I thought it might be prudent to perform a bit of research in reference to these "Indians' bones." In response to my inquiry, Mr. Whitacre of the State Department of Archives and History down there referred me to North Carolina General Statute 70, Article 3, The Unmarked Human Burial and Human Skeletal Remains Protection Act. Major provisions of the law are as follows: (You'll be most interested in #5.)

1. Legal protection of all unmarked human burials and human skeletal remains is provided.

2. Specific procedures to be followed when unmarked human burials and human skeletal remains are discovered are outlined.

3. Scientific excavation of unmarked human burials and human skeletal remains by professional archaeologists is allowed.

4. Provisions are made for scientific analysis of excavated remains and minimum qualifications for persons conducting scientific analysis.

5. The Executive Director, North Carolina Commission of Indian Affairs, in consultation with tribal groups, is given decision-

making authority with regard to ultimate disposition of Native American remains recovered (after completion of scientific analysis).

Mr. Whitacre called my attention to one more provision, namely, that 'Violation of the provisions of G.S. 70-37 is a Class H felony.' He also pointed out that, under the direction of the Commission of Indian Affairs, proper excavation of a sensitive site such as the one your "source" may have uncovered could take months or years. Mr. Whitacre further advised me that numerous construction projects, both public and private, have been postponed because of the statute's provisions.

—Sincerely,

Charles A. Chesterton, Chair,

Department of Cultural Anthropology

I checked the postmark—the letter had been in the mail the night Pogy died. There was something else in the envelope, something Melinda had stuffed in there while she was still on the ferry—the charred necklace that Shutterspeed had taken from around his dead friend's neck that night on Murdock's Island. She'd found it on the dashboard of the Chevy van, right where her suicide-bent lover had left it for her.

Over the next two weeks Melinda had to testify once for the Coast Guard inquiry and again at a coroner's inquest. The State of North Carolina was very unhappy about having a drowning death associated with its very own navy, even if it was ruled a clear suicide. News coverage was kept to a minimum, working out well for all of us.

I'm not too sure how hard they looked, but none of the

authorities in Carteret County or New York could locate any next of kin for Shutterspeed. But they found plenty of creditors.

The crab house owner, Clarence Rugby, somehow got the idea that he had become Shutterspeed's heir by default. After handing Melinda an inflated bill for back rent and other incidentals, Clarence put his own Master lock on the door and said he planned on selling the movie equipment. Against Melinda's protests, I went over there with Johnny to reclaim the gear that was rented on her credit card. A pair of long-handled Ridgid boltcutters made short work of the chain. With the equipment loaded in the van, I searched through the stacks of videotapes until I found the one I wanted. The rest we took to the dump.

The next day I went into Morehead City and showed Professor Chesterton's letter to the Croaker Neck Seafood League's chief lobbyist and money man, Ellis Vaughn, Attorney at Law.

"Call the Commission of Indian Affairs, the Department of History and Archives, and every TV station in the state," I said. "Tell them you've uncovered a violation of The Unmarked Human Burial and Human Skeletal Remains Protection Act. Then we'll go out to Murdock's Island and stop Oscar Cruz dead in his tracks."

"Why do I want to do that?"

"Number one, it will make the Croaker Neck Seafood League look like the most conservation-minded, Native American-friendly organization east of the Rockies."

"And number two?"

"It will keep Gus Ridge and his high-priced 'sportsmen' out of Core Sound for a little longer, and make developers like our friend Oscar think twice before they come this way again."

"You're right!" Ellis said, slapping his desk. "That peckerwood from Florida will flat lose his *ass* if that project stops."

"*When* it stops." I handed him the letter and laid a videotape on his desk. Reading the label, he got a sour look on his face.

"*Ilse Goes Shrimping*—what the hell's this for?"

"Make five copies of the ending," I told him. "In case we have any more trouble with Gus Ridge."

As soon as the inquiry into Shutterpeed's death was settled, Ilse and Melinda got into the crazily-painted Chevy with the overdue rental gear in the back and started for New York.

"I can't let that poor girl go alone," my favorite redhead told me. "And I think I need to get away from here for a while." Saying good-bye one more time.

Johnny came by the cabin for the send-off. Melinda insisted that she wanted to make a trade for Johnny's trademark Cat hat, and he handed it over. Nowadays he looks ridiculous culling shrimp in the harbor wearing a hat that says Panavision across the front.

After the van drove off we sat in my kitchen and had coffee. I wondered out loud how the cops on I-95 would react to the camo paint job, and we both laughed.

When the forced laughter was over I told him, "Ilse promised she'd come back."

"She will," Johnny said. He'd never lied to me before.

chaPter twenty

Agent Gatlin's case wasn't solved, exactly, but there was nothing he could use to bring charges against Melinda, so he'd let her go. He went back to his office in Carolina Beach, probably hoping he'd never hear another word from Croaker Neck again. But I still had his card with all those phone numbers, and figured that after all we'd been through together maybe I could get him to do me one last favor.

The next day Digger showed up at my cabin.

"Your cop friend called me last night," he said. "Told me he was a 'National Oceanic and Atmospheric Special Agent,' and that you had told him absolutely nothin' about anybody or anything in Croaker Neck."

"And?"

"You dumb bastard, you expect me to believe some turtle cop who thinks he's a secret agent?" I thought maybe he was going to haul off and jump ugly again, but then I realized he was just kidding. My feral old friend stood in front of me with his hand out, apologizing.

"Sorry, man. I went a little nuts for a while."

"A *little* nuts?"

"This whole town's been crazy, in case you didn't notice."

"Yeah, I noticed."

I shook his hand, told him no hard feelings. Then he told me we needed to take another boat ride up the Indian ditch. When I said, "No way," he promised me there'd be nothing illegal, that he just needed my help getting his duck blind ready for the season.

Duck season is serious business in Croaker Neck. As an obsession it surpasses fishing, which is after all, more of an occupation than a passion. Through the fall mullet blows, the spot runs, and the arrival of gray and speckled trout, the saltwater cowboy will keep fishing, shrimping, and catching oysters. But then one day, when the morning air has just the right edge of crispness, he'll drive his pickup truck off the highway and idle down a sandy track off into the woods. From there he'll return to the road, the truck bed piled high with fresh-cut brush—myrtle branches, reeds, bamboo—whatever he thinks it will take to make his duck blind invisible to the season's passing flocks.

On Saturday he'll haul his pickup load of natural camouflage down to the harbor and toss it onto his skiff. Taking along his best dog, a black or yellow Lab even more eager than he for the season to begin, he will carry the cut brush across the sound to his blind: a six-by-six wooden box that sits above the water on crooked pilings next to the marsh. The bits of brush and tufts of leaves are arranged with care against the weathered pine planking. Camouflage is his art, and he works with his boatload of materials until the blind is nothing more than another clump of vegetation invisible in the sea of marsh grass that is green and just starting to turn gold. When he's finished the artist and his Lab may climb up into the blind where he will picture just where the raft of decoys will sit, the perfectly natural way they will undulate with the waves. Looking up at his personal expanse of the Core Sound sky he and the dog will dream of redheads and bluebills gliding high, then turning at the sight of the decoys at their feet.

That golden ritual is what I had in mind as Digger's boat took us once again up into the Indian ditch. I had on a layer of fleece under my slicker, and it felt like it must have been long ago that we'd come this way with Pogy, and caught dolphin, and survived that wicked storm.

"Nothing illegal, right?"

"No sir. Just got to decorate my blind up yonder, is all." But when we got to a familiar spot near the end of the ditch Digger pulled the boat in against the shore and jumped out with a line. He tied us off and then reached back aboard for his Guatemala Toothpick. When I protested that he must be crazy, that he had promised no funny stuff, he said, "We're just going to cut some brush. Can't have a naked duck blind, can we?"

Through the cattails we went, inevitably then climbing a little through the woods to that bog on a hill. I was pretty sure what I was about to see, if not participate in, a major-league felony, but when we got into the pocosin there was no sign of agriculture at all. Not even a stalk.

"Where did it go?"

"You let me worry about that."

"Then you cut it? Even you can't smoke that much weed, so you must have sold it."

"Let's just say I've got it hid somewhere for safe keeping."

"You're nuts. What about getting your captain's license back? Hell, you won't be captain Davis—you'll be convict Davis."

"Dodge, you fret about things too much. Always have." And with that he very calmly started to cut branches from the bay myrtles around the pocosin's edge. "Come on, buddy, bundle these up so we can take them back to the boat." Without a clue what else to do, I started filling my arms with greenery.

We came out the north end of the ditch and into a narrow bay, the boat piled so high with myrtle that we must have looked like a floating thicket. I had hunted in Digger's blind a few times and knew its location, but when we got to the general area I became confused. As a matter of custom any duck hunter's traditional territory is respected by the locals, and buffers are maintained through common courtesy. But here, where Digger's had once been the only one in sight, there were now three new blinds crowding his flyway.

"Where did all this new stuff come from?" I asked.

"Funniest thing. I came up here last month and these boys were out here putting in pilings not fifty yards from my blind. Turns out they're a bunch of rich guys from Raleigh. One of the guides from Sea Level had brought them up here last season. They'd had good shooting, so they decided it was a great place to go on their own."

"Well I'll be damned!"

"Yeah, there was five or six of them, they had a big new camo-painted Carolina Skiff and a yellow Lab that looked for all the world like it didn't know how to swim. They claimed they'd gotten some kind of lease, but there's nobody I know who'd give them such a thing. Not right here."

"So what did you tell them, that they could all go to hell?"

"Why no, Dodge, that wouldn't be neighborly." Neighborly? I had to wonder if maybe Digger hadn't smoked so much Pocosin Poison that his mind wasn't right. For him to let a bunch of dingbatters crowd his duck hunting spot was something I couldn't imagine.

"Come on," he said, "let's get this brush on my blind and get back to the harbor." The fancy new blinds had yet to be camouflaged, but there was still a week until opening day. The Raleigh hunters would probably pay somebody to come out and get the blinds ready.

All the way back to Croaker Neck I pondered the new Digger. The old one would have tied a line to each one of those blinds and used the boat to drag them off into deep water one by one. The old Digger, in Johnny's words, had wanted to fish the blue water more than he wanted to breathe, but clearly he'd gone and rustled someone's field of pot and ruined his chances of ever getting clean enough to get his captain's license back.

The next Saturday was the opening day of the season. Oddly, that morning I saw Digger's Powerwagon parked at the minimart. Maybe the weather was a bit too nice for duck hunting, but it wasn't like him to miss opening day, especially with his blind all ready to go. Here was another chink in the armor of the salty captain I thought I knew so well.

The next morning he called and wanted to know if I'd seen the paper. What the hell was going on? Digger never read the newspaper.

"Why didn't you go up yonder yesterday, to hunt?" I asked.

"Quit playing Twenty Questions and go get the Sunday paper."

I drove over to the minimart and got the local rag. Digger's truck pulled into the lot just as I was reading the headline.

"Duck Hunters Decoyed In Pamlico Bust."

The day before, six hunters from Raleigh had been arrested in their duck blinds near Long Bay after a drug-sniffing dog aboard a Coast Guard boat on routine Homeland Security patrol got a whiff of a controlled substance on the wind. The Coasties radioed to a nearby Wildlife Patrol boat, then the warden and the orange inflatable raced across the sound, probably expecting that they would get a few laughs by scaring the hell out of some local teenagers smoking a joint. Imagine their surprise when they discovered over $20,000 worth of high-grade marijuana plants stapled, nailed, and tied to the outside of three otherwise ordinary duck blinds. A fourth blind in the area was adorned with the standard bay myrtle branches. The Raleigh men claimed that they had found the "camouflage" waiting for them in the blinds and assumed it was put there by the man who had leased them their section of marsh. Efforts to find the lease holder, or any record of the transaction, had proven unsuccessful.

Digger stood next to his truck laughing like a loon.

"We thought it was some kind of bamboo," the arrested hunters told authorities.

"Maybe they do come from so far *off* that they didn't know marijuana from bamboo," the paper quoted the Sheriff as saying.

"I'll admit it's possible, although I'm more inclined to believe these boys from the city thought they could put something over on us poor, plain folks Down East. About that they were sorely mistaken."

About the Author

Bill Morris has lived and written in Chapel Hill and Durham for the past eighteen years. He now splits time between the Triangle and Down East Carteret County, the setting for *Saltwater Cowboys*. A story adapted from this novel, "Dinah's Dog," won the 2003 Doris Betts Prize for Short Fiction. Other stories have been published in *Real Fiction, The Dead Mule, Urban Hiker, Spectator*, and the *Best of the O. Henry Festival 2003*. Morris, a graduate of Duke University, is also a regular contributor to *Our State* magazine, *Wildlife in North Carolina*, and the Raleigh *News & Observer* outdoors pages.